Back to Hell Country

A Balum Series Western
no.1

A novel by
Orrin Russell

1

Balum pulled up short before cresting the ridge. He didn't wish to skyline himself, and his horse had started to jerk at his bit the way it did when it smelled blood.

The idea that anyone was within miles of him at that moment was far-fetched. For three days he had been riding through scarred, broken country. Hell Country they called it. Water was scarce, as were human folk. Nonetheless, he dismounted and crawled the last few yards to the top of the ridge.

A hundred feet below, just a might further west, a man knelt on all fours. His arms made sweeping motions over the desert floor, scooping sand and rock into two piles as he excavated a hole by hand.

Balum lied down on his belly on top of the ridge. He pulled out a plug of tobacco and settled in to observe this strangeness.

A few yards from the digging man, a body lay face down. Balum watched the figure for some time and considered him dead. Deadman going into a hole in the desert. Only one horse though, and that didn't figure right. Neither did a large pine branch tied alongside the saddlebags.

Balum spat tobacco. What was this man doing with a pine bough tied to his horse in the middle of the desert, digging a hole by hand with a deadman in tow? He looked back to his own horse down the ridge. Hot, thirsty, and run ragged, the roan wasn't going anywhere. He turned back to the scene below.

The digger had gotten to his feet. He had the deadman by the arms. Into the hole he went, digger back to all fours, sand and rock pushed over the corpse. The digger stood and trudged back to the spot where the deadman had been sprawled over, and bent down.

Balum squinted.

The figure rose back up, this time holding two small bags.

Balum hadn't seen these.

The digger shoved them into his saddlebags. He unwound the pine bough and strapped it to the end of the saddle roll, allowing the needles to rest on the ground.

Balum had seen this trick before. It wouldn't wipe the tracks out completely, but with just a little help from the wind they would be gone before anyone came around to look.

The digger nudged the horse's rump forward a few

feet and inspected the trail. Satisfied, he mounted up and left the unmarked grave behind.

Balum spat again. The sun was going down and he didn't need any more trouble. He could ride in any direction at all. Riding after this fellow was asking for grief. No law-abiding man would bury people by hand in unmarked graves in the recesses of desert country. And no law-abiding man would ride with a pine bough track-concealer. But Balum also had a hunch what was in those bags. And without giving it any more thought, he mounted up and trailed after the digger.

Before long he was making camp. The sun was down and the cold was creeping in. His mystery man was somewhere ahead, and if he was making camp it was a fireless one just like Balum's.

He laid his head atop his saddlebags and eyed the stars. He wanted what was in those two bags. Filled with gold. Without a doubt. And when he got his hands on them he'd treat himself to a drink and a woman. Or two.

Morning had him up at daybreak. No fire, no breakfast, only a swig of water for him and the horse. If he didn't get out of this desert soon, that swig would be one of his last.

The digger's tracks showed up a couple miles ahead. He had discarded the pine concealer and evidently rode without any worry. Balum had missed the man's camp, though there might not have been much to it. He rode at a trot. Within the hour he caught up.

It didn't take long to spot him. Balum eased his pace and settled in a couple miles behind. He was headed to Bette's Creek, Balum was fairly certain of it. The only town in quite a few miles, it had sprung up like so many boomtowns do when talk of gold gets out: nearly overnight. Balum was fine with this. He had planned on stopping anyhow. Last week's trouble wasn't serious enough for anyone to cross the hell-baked country he had just been through, and where there was gold there were women, whiskey, and gambling.

How to get the gold off the digger though, now that was a question. He bit off a plug of tobacco and puzzled on this. Balum hadn't always toed the line where the law was concerned, but he had never dry-gulched a man for money either. Seems the digger was a murderer and a thief, but Balum couldn't be sure, and even if he was, it didn't set right. He spat and rode on. He wasn't the fastest thinker, but if he wrestled with something long enough he usually came up with an answer.

The sun was hot. Balum's water had run out, and the roan dragged its feet. Heat waves shimmered over the red clay, creating illusions on the horizon. When the digger turned his horse around and came charging back the way he had come, Balum thought this might be an illusion too.

It wasn't.

Balum dug his feet into the horse's ribs and bolted for a crag of upthrust rock.

When he reached it he jumped down and had the roan drop to its side. It obeyed, too tired to fuss. Balum peered over the rock and watched as the rider advanced. Looking far into the horizon, Balum could see what the digger must have seen. A dust cloud of riders.

When the digger got within fifty yards of Balum he jumped off his horse and yanked the two leather bags from his pack. He rushed to a rock slab overlaying a boulder and swung them into the gap. With a wild look back toward the dust cloud, he mounted and rode off at a gallop.

Balum waited. He fought against the urge to run out to the bags and grab them up. The group of pursuers was too close now. He could hear the hoofbeats and he swore he could feel the ground tremble as the animals' hooves drove into the earth. They came out of the shimmering heat waves in a burst, eight men riding hard. They rode within fifty yards of Balum. Their passing left a cloud of red-tinged dust in the air. Balum pulled his shirt collar up to his face and waited for it to settle. When it did, he crossed to the rock slab and took up the bags.

One heavy, one light. He opened the heavier one.

Gold. Pure nuggets, uniform in size, no dust or small specks at all. Just high quality gold.

He stomped a foot and leaned his head back. His

heart raced as he tore open the second bag. Inside were papers. He unfolded them and scanned them over.

One was a personal letter that held no interest to him. The other did. A deed to a mining claim. He read it over. Doug Bennett had signed it on the fourth day of March, 1867. It looked straight up, signed for by the Recorder and Deputy Recorder as witnesses for the County Records.

Balum could guess that Doug Bennett was the deadman who just got buried. He thought a moment. He could easily sign that claim over to himself. Just a matter of scrawling a similar likeness of the signature and releasing possession. He could write in a sale price. He'd have himself a mine worth stealing, without actually stealing.

He considered it a moment longer, then shoved the papers back into the pouch and threw it right back under the rock slab where he'd found it. Gold he would surely take, but evidence possibly linking him to the death of the digger's victim had no place in his pack.

His horse struggled to get back on its feet.

'Come on boy, let's go. There's water where we're going, and a stable waiting for you.'

He pocketed a few nuggets and shoved the rest into his saddlebag. Then he slid into the saddle and rode due west for Bette's Creek.

2

Bette's Creek was lively alright. Gunshots rang out as he approached the outskirts of town. Most likely just some drunk having fun, by the sound of it.

He didn't come in by the main road. Instead he skirted around to the south and came up through the back lanes, passing by some one-room houses of adobe and scattered tents that served as homes or places of temporary business.

The main drag was wide and dusty. It was lined with false-fronted stores, and in front of these were watering troughs for horses. Neither side even had a boardwalk, just dust and clay. His eyes passed over the view. He counted four good-sized saloons and a number of ramshackle lean-tos and even a couple tents that advertised the sale of liquor. There was a blacksmith, a few restaurants, two general stores, and three hotels. At the end of the street closest to where he stood was the livery stable.

The old-timer inside took the roan and led it to a

stall. Balum watched the wrinkled man fill the trough with water, a bucket with oats, then hang up the saddle and blanket.

'Sure enough is thirsty, ain't he?' said the livery man. Balum's horse had his head half buried in the water trough. 'Looks like he needed that drink.'

'He did,' said Balum. 'For that matter, so do I. What's the charge here?'

'Forty cents a night, and that includes water and feed.'

'Sounds right.' Balum reached into his vest pocket and brought out a small nugget. He passed it to the old-timer. 'Will that do for a few nights?'

'That'll do me all right!'

'That horse has been through hell with me. I want him given the royal treatment. I promised him quite a lot back yonder in Hell Country.'

'Yes sir, yes sir,' the man was grinning and staring at the small nugget. He looked up at Balum. 'You can trust me with your horse sir, he'll be happy here.' He pocketed the nugget. 'Looks like the mines have been good to you.'

'Luck's been good to me.'

'Ah, a gambling man. I think most of these fool gold hunters lose all their findings in the gambling halls.'

'I aim to see you're right. Now can you tell me where to find a quiet place to rest up for a few days? I'd like to try a roof over my head. These hotels on Main Street don't look like any place a man can find some quiet.'

'No sir, you're right about that. Just behind the Candelabra is a small guesthouse. Can't remember what it's called, but it's about the only place in this part of the country where you'll see fresh flowers hanging. Woman by the name of Charlise runs it.'

'What's the Candelabra?'

'What's the Candelabra? Well how the heck did you win that gold if you ain't even heard of the Candelabra? It's about the finest gambling you'll find here.'

'Thanks, old timer,' Balum tipped his hat.

'You watch out now, young man. Things here are known to turn violent real quick, and walking around with a pocket full of gold, why word gets out fast.'

Balum nodded.

'And go find that hotel I mentioned. I think you'll like what you see.'

The old man grinned, and as Balum exited the livery stable with his saddlebags over his shoulder, the smile only broadened.

When Balum stepped through the doors of the tiny hotel behind the Candelabra he understood the twinkle in the old man's eyes. Yeah, I like what I see, thought Balum.

In the small foyer was a reception desk, behind which Charlise stood scribbling in the books. She might have been thirty-five, and life had treated her well enough. She had a glow in her cheeks and silky hair that cascaded over her shoulders. She was dressed in something closer to what you'd see in a whorehouse than a respectable establishment. Her dress was tied tightly around her waist, and came up to hold two massive breasts. They were pushed up and together, making a deep tight cleavage of white creamy skin. The tops of them jiggled as she wrote in her books, and Balum felt his blood pump as he took her in.

Charlise looked up at him when he approached the desk. Her face changed from neutral to mild disgust in an instant.

'Looking for a room,' he said.

'Rooms here cost money. Looks like you came in off the street.'

Balum looked down at his outfit. She was right. He'd been a week without a bath. His clothes were stained with red desert chalk, and sweat had left dark streaks that stained his shirt. He was unshaven, and surely didn't smell too good either.

'In that case I'll take a bath as well.'

She crossed her arms just under her chest, pushing her massive tits even higher. Balum wondered if she knew the effect this produced. There was something about him that brought out her snobbish side.

He took out a gold piece. When the woman's eyes saw it they lit up momentarily. She pursed her plump lips together and reached out for it, but he held back.

She scowled. 'I'm not a good judge of gold value, mister. You'd be better off to change that into cash at the gold buyer's station.'

'I'll be sure to do that, but for now it's all I've got.'

He handed it over. She took the nugget from him and put it in her register.

'Now how much for that room?'

'A room runs two dollars a night, and a bath is a quarter dollar.'

'How much with you in it?'

'I beg your pardon?'

'How much for you in that bath with me?'

'How dare you! I am a married woman,' she stammered, obviously flustered. She placed her hands on her hips and took a defiant stance.

'Well I ain't taken no vows ma'am. And when a man's been on the trail as long as I have, a good-looking woman like yourself gets his blood to flowin.'

'I'll try to take that as a compliment. But I suggest you'd be better served at one of the brothels in town. God knows there are enough of them. Maybe some desperate girl will satisfy you there.'

She was mad alright. Her eyes pierced through him. She stood with her back straight and her chest out. He wanted to grab her right there and feel her soft lips on his, taste her mouth with his tongue. He also knew that as riled up as she was, he was closer to spending the night in a local jail cell than one of her rooms. So he shut his mouth and took his room key and, with a departing smile, left her standing behind the reception desk, flustered and indignant.

His room was small but clean. A bed, a table next to it, a small chair by the window. The interior was dark. As his eyes adjusted he noticed something peculiar. One of the plywood walls separating the rooms had several small holes in it. He walked up to the wall and looked through a hole. On the other side was an empty room much like his. He didn't like the idea of anyone spying on him.

He searched around the room for a quick fix. The wooden bedframe had several loose nails sticking out. He wiggled a couple free, then smacked them into the hole-ridden wall with the butt of his gun and strung the bedsheet to them. He stepped back and admired his work. It would stop any nosy neighbors from looking in on him at least.

When his bath had been run he crossed to the washroom and dipped into the hot water. He scrubbed the desert grime from his body and felt the tension in his muscles drift away. He shaved in the small mirror and, once back in his room, put on his only other pair of clothes. They weren't exactly fresh-pressed, but they made a difference.

He took the gold bag from his gear and stuffed it into his trouser pockets.

When he descended the staircase into the reception area, the woman at the desk scarcely recognized him. Balum wasn't the most handsome man. His face was battered by a life under the sun, and several fistfights had left his nose slightly bent. But he had a strong jaw and thick shoulders, and stood taller than average. He'd learned over the years that from time to time women would get into heat just like any other animal, and when lustful enough, it was to his type that some of them looked for satisfaction.

He left his room key with the Charlise on the way out. She took it without speaking to him. He could see she was slightly confused. She didn't much like him, but there was something about his look and the way he carried himself that made her want to find out more. She wanted to argue with him and put him in his place. Balum could read her like he could read a horse, or a tinhorn at a poker table.

He left her just as he had before, flustered and indignant.

3

Balum needed to change his gold into cash, but he also needed a steak and a beer. Grudgingly, he admitted that food could wait.

The gold buyer had set up shop right next to the sheriff's office. Not a bad idea, thought Balum. Outside the office stood eight hard-ridden horses. A crowd of bystanders milled around, chattering amongst themselves. He could guess what the fuss was about.

He walked into the crowd and listened in on the gossip. Sure enough, they had gotten their man. The bullet-ridden body hung face-down over the saddle of the horse he used to own. Balum recognized both the horse and the digger laying over its back. The gossip swirling amongst the townsfolk was about stolen gold and its whereabouts. Sure, the posse had come back with the thief, but they hadn't gotten the gold.

Two men with shotguns stood at the door of the gold buyer's shop. When Balum approached, one of them spoke up.

'Customer inside. He won't be long if you don't mind waiting a minute or two.'

'I don't mind,' replied Balum, his stomach growling.

'God almighty, I can hear that rumbling from here,' laughed the guard. 'You better get some grub in you.'

'I aim to.' Balum looked over the crowd. 'Seems like a lot of fuss over a thief.'

'Well, that thief didn't rob just anybody. Damn fool stole it from the sheriff's daughter. First week's cache out of her claim.'

'The sheriff's daughter has a mining claim?'

'Man, just about ever'body here has got gold fever. Yep, she's got her own claim all right. And from word around town, that mine actually produces.'

'Had a claim,' the other guard, silent until now, spoke up.

'What's that?' said the other.

'She ain't got no legal claim on that mine no more. Papers got stolen too.'

The door opened suddenly, and a miner exited. The guard motioned Balum inside.

The office was simple. Aside from the large steel safe in the corner, the only furniture consisted of a desk with a chair in front of it and another one behind. In this one sat the gold buyer.

'Good afternoon sir. I hope you're here to buy gold, not sell it.'

'No sir, I was aiming to sell.'

'You and just about everybody else in town. Mister,

I've got bad news for you, I'm fresh out of cash. There's a Wells Fargo stage coming in tomorrow and I'll be more than happy to assist you when it does. I pay $22.50 to the ounce.'

Balum tried to do the math in his head. He guessed he had two pounds total. Somewhere over $700 dollars just sitting in his pocket.

Before their conversation went further, the door flew open. The knob slammed into the wall. Balum jumped, startled, his hand naturally dropping to grasp the butt of his gun. He never liked having his back to a door.

Turning around, his level of surprise only increased. Stampeding into the room was a young woman. She wore a thin blue dress that clung to every curve of her body, and heeled riding boots that clapped loudly on the hardwood flooring. She marched straight up to the desk and stood right next to Balum, ignoring him completely.

'Mr. Elsworth, I thought my father was clear with you about continuing business after all that has happened.'

Her voice was nasally and each word was drawn out with a pampered whine. Balum remained seated. His eyes focused on the pert round ass scarcely concealed by the thin dress. It clung so finely to her thighs it seemed he could ascertain their firmness as if he was gripping them in his own hands.

'Yes Ms. DeLace, your father and I spoke. You must understand though, I have a business to run here, and many people in this town do as well. They all need to be able to sell their gold and carry on.'

'This is unacceptable. Any person selling gold who doesn't own a mine should be questioned.'

'Ma'am, plenty of people who don't own mines come into gold through honest methods.'

'That is nonsense. What's the nature of this man's business for example?' she motioned to Balum. 'What is his honest method?'

At this Balum stood up. His body was only inches from hers, and he looked down at her upturned face. She was worked up. Her eyes were angry and her haughtiness did not diminish at all as she stared Balum in the eye.

'Miss,' he said, 'you're rude. You've interrupted a private meeting and I'll kindly ask you to leave until we are finished.'

It was as if he'd slapped her across the face. Her mouth dropped open and she took a step back. She inhaled quickly, her small breasts rising in the thin cloth material. 'How dare you speak to me that way! Do you have any idea who I am?'

'Lady I could give a damn. I haven't eaten in two days, haven't slept much in a week, and what I care about now is a steak dinner and some rest. Now you've just insinuated that I'm a thief and I don't take kindly to that. If you were a man you might be dead already. But looks to me like you're just a spoiled child, so I'll have you leave here, and I'd advise you to pick up some manners before you come back.'

'Wha, wha...,' she stammered. 'Mr. Elsworth...'

'The door,' Balum pointed his hand to it.

The gold buyer said nothing. He had lived in Bette's Creek for nearly a year, and he knew that the DeLace family practically ran the town. And Deborah DeLace was certainly not used to this kind of treatment.

She turned and walked to the door. Her heels struck the floor a blow at each step. At the door she turned and faced Balum. 'What is your name?' she asked in her nasally moan of a voice.

'The name's Balum. A pleasure to meet you.'

She stiffened. His cavalier attitude was unlike any she had experienced before. 'You will be hearing from me shortly, Mr. Balum,' she said, and exited the shop.

Balum swung the door shut behind her and turned back to Elsworth. 'So no sale until tomorrow. That's what you're saying?'

'That's correct, sir. By noon, as long as the stage isn't held up.'

Balum tipped his hat. 'I'll be seeing you tomorrow then.'

4

The Independent Saloon had a choice position on the main drag. It was the largest and most elegant of the establishments in Bette's Creek. Of course, thought Balum, what passed for elegant in a pop-up boomtown. It didn't have the scale of gambling the Candelabra had, but it drew in the high society folk.

Before ordering, he pulled out a gold nugget. He gave it to the waiter and told him he wanted a tab run. The waiter raised his eyebrows at the nugget and assured Balum that it would get him more than just one meal. With that he ordered up a steak and a beer. When the steak arrived and the smell of the meat hit him he realized just how worn out he was. He'd been on the trail too long, and had missed too many meals. The desert had taken its toll on him, and as he ate, he felt his strength come back.

Halfway through the steak he ordered another beer. It was cold with a frothy head and it went down easy. As he shoveled in the steak, the door of the

Independent opened and a large mustached man wearing a badge entered. Just behind him came a tall skinny type with thin lips and a nervous look to him. He also wore a badge. Close behind this one was Deborah DeLace. She wore more ladylike attire at the moment. Balum realized that she must have rushed over to the sheriff's office wearing that thin blue dress in a hurry when the posse had come back. Even so, no dress could hide her swollen young ass and firm tits. She was the type of woman folks stood aside for, and Balum knew why.

The three of them scanned the room and Deborah spied him. She voiced something to her father and pointed in Balum's direction. They approached his table. The sheriff took off his hat.

'Balum, is it?'

'That's right.'

'I'm Henry DeLace and I'm the sheriff here in Bette's Creek. This here is Lance Cain: deputy.'

Balum nodded his head in acknowledgment while he chewed.

'My daughter says you spoke roughly to her in Elsworth's shop.'

'Your daughter accused me of being a thief. I don't take that lightly.'

'That true Deborah?'

'I did no such thing!' the girl cried. Her words were drawn out in a way Balum found quite sensual. Her nasally voice was the type that would sound good while moaning.

'My daughter is upset and so am I,' continued DeLace. 'We have a working claim that was robbed just two days ago. They took off with about the same weight of gold you offered to sell Elsworth. I'm sure you can understand her concern.'

'Sheriff, I pulled into this town this morning. Never set eyes on it before. So I ain't your man and don't cotton to gettin' my ass rode over nothin'.'

'You'll watch your language around the lady, Balum. You might not be the man we're looking for, but there's plenty of shenanigans happening around this town that have got folks upset. The Candelabra has been coming up short, we've had six shootings this week alone, claim jumpers, thefts out of hotels, you name it. And a man who rides into town out of nowhere with two pounds of gold in his pocket talking loosely to my daughter makes a mark in my book.'

Balum wasn't eating his steak anymore. His temper flared. With two beers in his dehydrated frame it was all he could do to keep from palming the Colt Dragoon revolver from its holster. He still had some sense in him though. Sheriff DeLace was a tough man, but Balum could handle him. It was the deputy that had Balum worried. The way he stood there staring silently at Balum, something was wrong with that man.

The sheriff placed a hand on the table and leaned in. 'I've been asking around about you, Balum. Seems no one can account for you,' he paused. 'Now I've gone and interrupted you at meal time. I'll let you finish. But I've still got several questions for you. I expect to have them answered in my office tomorrow morning. If you don't show up, I'll assume you're hiding something. I'll have to send Lance after you.'

The deputy stretched his thin lips into a smile and curled his boney fingers over the butt of his six gun.

Balum gripped the edge of the table and looked at the sheriff. Behind him Deborah grinned defiantly, her hand on her ample hips. She relished seeing him put in his place by her father.

'I've got my eye on you, Balum. And I'll give you a friendly warning. The longer you stay in Bette's Creek, the more likely it is you'll end up in my jail cell or at the end of a rope.'

Before Balum could muster a response, the sheriff and his deputy turned and left. With a last steely look at Balum, Deborah did the same.

5

Balum swore to himself quietly as he walked back to his lodging. As unlikable as Deborah and her father were, that gold rightfully belonged to them. That bothered him. No, he hadn't stolen it from them, but now that he had it, would he do the right thing and give it back? His mind tossed this over as he opened the hotel door and entered the lobby. What he saw thankfully took his mind off that unpleasant matter.

At the receptionist desk stood the proprietress, wearing another sultry top that showed off her enormous tits. This one was not so low-cut, but it was tighter than the last, and it cupped both juggs firmly out in front of her body.

In front of the counter a couple was registering. The man was fat and past middle-aged, dressed in fine Eastern clothing and reeking of money. The woman with him caused Balum to stop short and swallow. She had thick wavy hair and a massive rear end that seemed to defy gravity.

When Balum entered she turned and looked, her eyes shamelessly taking him in from head to toe. He decided it was only fair for him to do the same, so he scanned her over, taking his time on her large ass. She gave him a smile and sashayed her hips for him, her great ass bobbing from one side to the other. Balum felt his cock bulge in his pants.

He had run across this type of woman before. Whoever this man with her was, he had most likely picked her up from some whorehouse back East. Her clothing and composure said it all. She had found a man with money, and this was the type of woman that needed to be with the buck stallion. She wanted to be next to the man who cut the widest swath. So now she had the money, but with this old fat man she was missing something else she needed. She saw it in Balum.

While the gentleman droned on with Charlise, Balum and the whore gazed at each other. She smiled, turning about slowly and showing off her wares. Without thinking, his hand dropped to his pants to adjust his bulging package. Her eyes followed the movement and she looked him in the eye and licked her lips.

The man finally finished the check-in process and the two turned to the stairs. As they ascended, she brushed her dress smooth over her ass cheeks and gave one last smile to Balum.

When Balum turned to Charlise he was so flustered he had nothing to say. Nothing had been lost on the receptionist. She had seen the way the two flirted with each other, and something about it upset her. She spread her arms wide on the countertop and lifted her head slightly, showing off her soft neck.

'May I help you?' she asked.

'Ah yes, of course. Pardon. My room key, please.'

She took it from its place on the key rack and handed it to him.

He left without so much as a 'thank you', and climbed the staircase to his room. Once inside he tossed his gold on the bed, took off his holster and jacket and slipped off his boots. He put his hands to his head and ran them through his hair.

It was all too much. Charlise and her giant rack, Deborah, the beers from the Independent, and now this fat whore with her succulent ass just wiggling it in front of him shamelessly. It was driving him crazy. He went to the wall and slipped the sheet from the nails. He put his nose to it and looked through one of the small holes.

What luck! The couple had been given the room next to his. The man was just leaving, and Balum heard the footsteps taking him to the washroom. The woman began to unlace her dress, and when all the ribbons were untied she let it fall from her body. Underneath she wore a corset tied tightly around her waist, two large cups supporting her breasts. She wore white lace panties which she began to slide down her thighs. Large, meaty thighs. Balum wished he was between them.

When she had taken them off she turned to place them on the bed stand. Her ass was larger than he could have believed, completely smooth and round, the skin taut and shiny. She sat down on the edge of the bed, then wet her fingers in her mouth and began to rub her pussy. She lifted one leg up onto the edge of the bed and let out soft moans while she fingered herself.

Balum dropped his trousers and stroked his engorged cock. Common sense had left him. In the dilapidated wall separating them was a larger hole just below his waist. With a distant thought that told him he shouldn't, he slid his cock through the hole. As soon as he did, the whore took notice and gasped, closing her legs abruptly and covering her mouth with her hand.

She looked around as if there might be someone else about, then looked back at Balum's dick protruding from the wall. She stood up from the bed and approached it. Balum watched her eagerly from his peephole, his body pressed against the wall. With her fingers she lightly stroked his shaft, then knelt to her knees and slid her tongue over the length of it. Having warmed up to the idea, she took it in her mouth and sucked, wetting it with her warm saliva. She rubbed her pussy while she sucked it, closing her eyes and letting out little moans.

She stood suddenly, and with her back to the wall, she bent over at the waist. She reached back and grasped his cock, backing up slowly and sliding it gently into her soaking wet cunt. She began to rock her giant ass up against the wall and back, over and over, her pussy lips sliding back and forth along Balum's shaft.

Balum could hear her moans growing, and suddenly she rammed her ass back into the wall, sending his cock deep into her pussy. He felt her tighten and she moaned out in orgasm, her hands braced on her knees, her body shuddering. She then pulled forward, stood up, and walked to the bed. With a smile on her face she climbed onto the mattress and stretched out, leaving Balum trembling up against the wall, watching.

He had lost all sense of reason. How could she leave him like this? He was ready to explode. Vaguely realizing how stupid this might be, he slid his dick out from the hole and opened his room door. The hallway was clear. He tiptoed out and reached for the neighboring door handle. It turned and he threw the door open.

The whore popped up in bed. Balum flung the door closed behind him and in just a few steps he was beside the bed. She drew her legs up and turned around, preparing to crawl off the far side of the bed, but Balum was quick. He grabbed her waist from behind with both hands and dragged her across the mattress to him. She was on all fours, her ass directly in front of Balum.

'Ohh!' she cried out.

Balum wrapped one arm fully around her belly and with his other hand grabbed his cock and rammed it deep into her still soaking wet pussy.

'Oooooh,' she cried out again.

He spread one of her ass cheeks aside with his free hand and watched his throbbing dick pound her snatch. His balls slapped against her and his hips plowed into her fat rear-end. She turned her head to look at him, her mouth open, her eyebrows slightly raised.

Balum felt his balls tightening. Closing his eyes, he thrust his shaft deep into her crevice. His hand gripped her ass so hard she let out a cry, and he felt his dick erupt its load inside her. He gave her a few final pumps and slid out. She collapsed onto the mattress and rolled over, her legs spread open with his cum spilling out of her and running down her meaty thighs.

'Oh my God,' she muttered, and rubbed her cum-covered pussy with her fingers.

With the release, Balum had come to his senses. He took one last look at her then turned for the door. In an instant he was back in the safety of his room. He threw the slide bolt on the door and fell into bed. Within moments he was asleep.

6

He didn't sleep well. He was restless. Before the sun broke the horizon he had his boots on. He knew what was bothering him; it was that damn gold. He should give it back to its rightful owners, no matter that he couldn't stand them. He also needed to think of a reason for why he still had it.

He left his room. At the bottom of the stairs he nearly tripped. Behind the receptionist's desk sat a spitting image of Charlise, only half her age. Not only did she have the same full lips and silky hair, but she had a pair of tits as enormous as her mother's.

Balum forgot all about the gold and smiled at the young lady.

'Well good morning to you, beautiful. I don't believe we've met.'

She stood up and smiled, 'Good morning, my name is Cynthia. You must be Mr. Balum.'

'That's right. How did you know?'

'My mom told me about you. She said not to talk to

you.'

'Looks like you're already disobeying orders.'

She giggled. 'I'm a grown girl, I can do whatever I want.'

'And what do you want to do?'

'I don't know,' she said, smiling. She leaned onto the reception counter with her elbows, one finger in the corner of her mouth. She wore the same type of dress her mother did. Her giant firm breasts were smashed together and came spilling out over the top.

Balum eyed them hungrily. 'I do,' he said.

She laughed, and this caused them to bounce. 'Maybe Mommy was right.'

'I suspect she was,' Balum said, and handed his room key over. He tipped his hat and left. If he had stayed any longer he didn't know if he could have resisted reaching out and grabbing a handful of soft breast.

He didn't want to see the sheriff. Not one bit. He decided instead to check on his horse. The way things were starting to shape up, he might need it in a hurry.

The livery stable was quiet but the doors were open. Balum walked in and saw the old timer going about his morning chores. When he noticed Balum he smiled.

'I was wondering about you. Did you end up making it to Charlise's place?'

'I did.'

'Suit you alright?' the old man said with a grin.

Balum nodded knowingly. The two men laughed.

'She says she's married,' said Balum.

'She is. Her husband drives the long route stage. He's gone weeks at a time.'

'Sounds like a lonely life.'

'For her or for the stage driver?' the old man asked, and they both chuckled again. 'The name is Chester, by the way.'

'Balum.'

'Balum. The man who rode in from Hell Country. Folks have been talking about you, Balum.'

'Is that right?'

'Seems you gave Deborah DeLace a piece of your mind. That Elsworth, his lips get to flappin. And people are talking about how the sheriff scolded you right in public. They say it was like a schoolmaster reprimanding a student.'

Balum felt anger growing inside him. He didn't like people knowing his business. 'I don't care for your sheriff much,' he said.

'Well that makes two of us.'

'Yeah?'

'Let me tell you something, youngster,' said Chester. He had put his watering pail down and pulled out a plug of chewing tobacco. He offered some to Balum and they both stuck a wad in their cheeks. 'Bette's Creek has been around a long time,' he continued. 'I've been here most of twenty years. Started out a fair sized town, but the railroad never came and people moved on. Town died just a little more with each year. Got to be there weren't more than forty, fifty people to the place. Wasn't much of a town. Just a lot of big empty buildings. Now there must be five thousand. That's all happened in the last year. Gold did it.' He spat tobacco juice on the ground.

'Henry DeLace came in right before it boomed. Come in with his daughter, and a shabby looking lot they were. Dust bowl misery if I ever saw it. As luck would have it, that first gold nugget was discovered less than a week after they rode in. Word got out and in came the prospectors. Then the businessmen, the gamblers, the gunslingers, the whores, and everyone else. Town being so small like it was, we didn't have no sheriff. So he went ahead, put a star on his chest, and wham. There's your sheriff.'

'You mean nobody ever elected him?'

'Nope. Then he goes and starts charging *licensing fees*. Stands out on the end of Main Street and charges a dollar for every man, woman and child that rides in. Says it's a city ordinance. Hires that killer Lance Cain to back him up.'

'I'll be damned,' whistled Balum.

'Goddamn crook is what he is! And this cockamamie story over the claim,' Chester shook his head. 'I don't know where it's all gonna end.'

'What about the claim?'

'That claim don't belong to his daughter any more than it does me. That claim was old Doug Bennett's, and once he found gold, why...'

Balum hung on the old man's words. 'Go on,' he said, spitting tobacco into the dirt.

'Story turns strange from there. Mostly hear-say. Only thing folks agree on is that Deborah DeLace shows up at Bennett's claim just before sunset one night. She's in his cabin and shots are fired. Then guess what. The place burns down. Sheriff comes over, don't let nobody near it. He sets off a stick of dynamite right where the cabin set up against a ledge. Ruble buries the cabin. And that's old Doug Bennett's resting place.'

Balum shook his head and spit more tobacco juice into the dust. His mind worked over this new information. 'How can Deborah say she owns the claim? And what about the gold thief they went after in Hell Country? The sheriff led that posse himself.'

'Deborah says she bought the claim from Bennett. She explains away the gunshots saying he was drunk and celebrating the sale. Now those claim papers are burned up. You try contradicting that young lady's story and her old man is likely to stretch your neck out with a rope.' Chester had started up with his chores again. Balum followed behind as he pitched forks of hay into the stalls.

'That gold thief,' continued Chester. 'Now there's a mystery. That was a no good bum DeLace used to hang around with before he made hisself sheriff. Jed, I think his name was. Those two are tied up in this, I just can't figure as to how. But now Jed's dead, and DeLace is the one who shot him. So good luck figuring that one out.'

Balum's head felt foggy. Chester had given him a lot to chew on, and all on an empty stomach. He thanked the livery man for the tobacco and the straight talk and headed out for some grub.

7

With his belly full of beans and eggs and coffee to boot, he began to make his way down the main drag toward the sheriff's office.

The only certainty he'd come to over breakfast was that he wasn't so keen to hand the gold over to DeLace anymore. He'd been feeling guilty, and now that feeling was gone. He didn't want any more trouble, and maybe by sitting down with the sheriff he could smooth things over.

Then again, deeper down, he knew what he should do was grab his gold and ride. Get the hell out.

Then why was he sticking around? For one more look at Charlise? A chance with her daughter? Dammit. He was a fool.

He knocked on the sheriff's door. Lance Cain opened it, his thin lips stretching over yellow teeth in a grimace that served as a smile.

Henry DeLace sat in a swivel chair behind a wooden desk. Behind him were three empty jail cells, each containing a cot and a bucket to piss in. A shiver went through Balum.

'Bring back bad memories, Balum?' the sheriff laughed. 'Sit down.'

Balum took a seat in front of the desk. He didn't like the feeling of Lance Cain standing behind him.

The sheriff leaned forward and crossed his thick arms over the desk. He had lost his smile. 'Bette's Creek is my town. I run it. I keep it safe, and I make sure that law is upheld. Anybody coming in to stay puts up a licensing fee of one dollar. That goes to law and order, and to civic matters. That applies to you. You don't like it, you can leave.'

Balum said nothing.

'There's been plenty of trouble lately. Someone's stealing from the Candelabra, miners are quarreling over gold, and my own daughter has been robbed. Most of these claims are just producing flakes, hers were uniform nuggets. Two pounds of them. I've let Elsworth the Gold Buyer know to alert me to anyone selling nuggets,' his eyes squinted at Balum. 'Down at the Independent they say you started a tab with a nice looking gold nugget. I'll warn you right now. Any man caught with two pounds of gold in nugget form will end up in one of these.' He pointed to the three cells. 'And after a couple nights in there I'll give him a necktie made of rope.'

Balum nodded. He had thought he might smooth things out with the sheriff. He was wrong. 'I hope you find your man,' said Balum, and he stood up.

Lance stood by the door. His hand twitched nervously next to his gun. He hesitated, then opened the door for Balum.

Once out on the street he took a few large breaths. That had done it. No need of staying past the morning. He'd have a drink, take one more look at Charlise and Cynthia, and be gone by sunrise. He liked his neck just the way it was. Stretching it out wouldn't serve him any better.

That meeting had rattled him. DeLace suspected he had something to do with the stolen gold, and Lance Cain was a harebrained killer. Balum's nerves were on edge. He had been elated when he found that gold, and had made plans of drinking, gambling and womanizing. Now all of that had turned around.

He could use a drink.

His credit was still running at the Independent, and he went there now. The waiter from yesterday recognized him and served him up a cold mug of beer. Balum drank greedily. He ordered another and felt the cool liquid run down his throat.

It bothered him that a couple of murdering thieves were going to get the best of the town. Deborah had most likely murdered that man Bennett, and her father knew it. They sent their friend Jed off to bury the body in Hell Country, only in the commotion they didn't realize that Bennett had the gold and the claim on his person.

Balum ordered another beer. The more he drank, the more the picture cleared up. Once Deborah and her father had wised up to what had happened, they sent a posse out to find Jed. Seems maybe there wasn't too much trust between thieves. But they hadn't found the gold, or the deed to the claim. All they'd done was succeeded in killing Jed, the only other man in on the crime.

Balum congratulated himself. Maybe he should have been a pinkerton, he thought, and chuckled.

The waiter came back to check on his table.

'Get me another beer. And a shot of good whiskey!' Balum's voice boomed. He was getting drunk, and he liked the feeling.

When the whiskey came he threw it back and chased it with a swig of fresh beer. His mind drifted to the fat-assed whore in the room next to him. He wondered if she was still there. But she was nothing compared to Charlise and her daughter Cynthia. By God they had the most amazing racks. It was so rare to find such large breasts that didn't sag, but instead perked up firm and round. He could imagine just what they looked like naked.

He gulped down the last of the beer and walked into the street. The sun was bright overhead and he squinted, stumbling past the horses tied to the hitching posts, around the corner of the Candelabra, up to the hotel.

Upon opening the door he entered into the very same scene from the day before. Charlise was behind the reception counter, in conversation with the pudgy easterner. His voluptuous wife stood behind him, waiting.

Charlise looked up and scowled immediately. She could tell he was drunk by the way he was weaving and by the sly grin on his face. The whore looked at him as well, startled. She remembered all too well yesterday's adventure, and she blushed upon seeing him.

Balum attempted to temper his actions. He put his hands in his trouser pockets and slowly approached the front desk. The easterner was inquiring about stage times and how his luggage would be transferred if he missed a connection. His wife stood behind him, and as Balum approached she turned her head a bit and watched him out of the corner of her eye.

He stopped just behind her and stood in line. Looking forward over her shoulder and over the head of her husband, he gazed at Charlise. She looked up at him while the easterner rambled on, and her lips pressed together in disapproval. Balum returned her stare, and as he did so, his hips unconsciously pressed forward into the huge round ass of the whore. The woman looked back, her eyes wide and surprised, then she smiled and turned forward again. With one hand she reached behind her and began to stroke Balum's cock through his trousers.

Balum sighed and felt his head lighten. While the whore stroked his growing member, he continued to exchange eye contact with Charlise. He watched her big breasts shake while she pointed out itineraries on the stage schedule. He wanted to slide his cock over them and have her full lips wrapped around it. He was so aroused he nearly grabbed the whore by her waist and dry humped her from behind. But the easterner had gotten the information he needed and the couple left.

Balum was left standing in front of the reception counter, drunk and staring at Charlise.

'Yes, Mr. Balum, may I help you?' asked Charlise, clearly annoyed.

'Mmm, I'd love some help,' he grinned.

She looked down and saw the obvious bulge in his pants. She caught her breath. Her mouth parted. 'Oh my.'

Balum gripped his swollen member through his pants and accommodated himself.

'You have some nerve, you know,' said Charlise, although Balum sensed some of her annoyance had turned to something else. 'Your original payment will take you through tonight, but then you'll either have to check out, or pay up again,' she said, making an attempt at professionalism. Her continued staring at Balum's crotch though, gave away where her mind was at.

'How about I make a payment right now?' he slurred. He reached across the counter and cupped one of her giant tits in his hand.

'Mr. Balum!' she cried out, and slapped his hand away. 'You're drunk. Now go to your room and behave yourself. If my husband were to come in and see you groping me he'd call the sheriff!'

At the mention of the word *sheriff* Balum came to

his senses. He drew away from the desk, picking up the room key Charlise had laid out. 'I'll see you later,' he said, and climbed the stairs.

Charlise watched him go. Her face was red. She felt hot, and although she told herself he was a no-good drifter, she couldn't deny the fact that her panties were slightly wet.

8

Balum barely made it to the bed before he passed out. He slept deeply. He dreamt of Deborah DeLace, of her thin dress and her air of superiority. He dreamt of her scolding the townsfolk, reprimanding them in the town square. She reprimanded Charlise, and Charlise tore her top off and licked her nipples in response. He dreamt of the deadman in Hell Country, of gold scattered all about and horse hooves pounding into red clay.

He woke up confused. For a moment he didn't know where he was, nor the time of day. The sun was low in the sky. Sundown. He swung his feet to the floor and rubbed his eyes. One last night in Bette's Creek and then he would be riding the trail again. This time though, with two years' worth of cowhand's wages in his pocket.

He had passed out fully clothed. He ran his hands down his shirt to smooth out the wrinkles. Then he opened the saddlebag where he had stored his cache of gold. He dug through it and came up short.

Where had he put that bag? Dammit, he thought, this is what happens when a man gets to drinking. He searched through the saddlebag again, then unfurled his bed roll. He turned out his other set of clothes, dirt-stained and stinking. The pockets were empty. He ripped the covers from the bed, his heart rate rising. His eyes darted around the small room, searching the corners, but the room was just as sparse and empty as usual.

He dropped to his knees and went through all his possessions more slowly, thoroughly checking every piece of material with desperate intensity. He owned so little. It didn't take much time to go through it.

The gold was gone.

Balum stood up. His head ached from the beers and whiskey. He felt a sinking in his stomach and his legs weakened. He sat on the bed, his mind numb.

He began to work over the events of the last couple days. Who had access? Had the whore next door or her husband seen him through the holes in the wall? No, he had rehung the sheet. What about in that brief moment when he had gone to her room? He had left his door unlocked. Who would have entered? Maybe Charlise. Or her daughter. Could he trust them? They could enter at any moment, after all. They had keys.

Somehow that didn't fit. Their interactions with him gave away no sense of guilt. But who else?

He put his boots on, slowly. He buckled his gunbelt around his waist and went to the washroom. He splashed cold water on his face from the bucket on the sink and rubbed the sleep from his eyes. He didn't know what he was going to do, but he needed to do something.

Descending the staircase, he came upon Cynthia at the front desk. As beautiful as the young lady was, and as revealing as tonight's outfit was, he was in no mood for games.

'Hello, Mr. Balum,' she smiled.

Balum grunted in response.

'My mom said to remind you that you've only paid through tonight. Check out tomorrow is at 9:00am.'

'I know, I know,' he growled, and tossed his room key on the counter.

'My, you're in a sour mood today.'

'You're goddamn right I am.' He scowled at her, but it was hard to be ornery while looking at such a beautiful face, and those giant luscious breasts heaving over the rim of her dress.

She saw where his eyes were going and she brushed her hair back for him to get a better view. As she did so her fingers grazed the top side of her tits. 'I wish I could make you feel better,' she purred.

He leaned against the desk, inches away from her, and looked down onto her massive cleavage. Her face turned up to him, her red lips parted ever so slightly. 'Is there anything I can do, Mr. Balum?'

'How about you--,' Balum's words were cut short by the door behind the receptionist area swinging open. Charlise stepped through. At the sight of Balum and

Cynthia so close, she frowned.

'Cynthia, it's about time you got going.'

'Yes mother.'

'Balum? Will you be extending your stay or have we seen the last of you?'

'Haven't decided yet,' he mumbled. This was the first time he had seen Charlise and Cynthia together at the same time. They looked strikingly similar. They both loved to show off their breasts. It almost seemed they were in a contest to see who could shove more flesh out of the tops of their dresses. He couldn't decide which one he wanted more. He wanted them both.

Cynthia left through the same door her mother had come through, giving her ass an extra wiggle as she did so. Balum watched her go and turned back to Charlise.

'I'll give you a piece of advice if you'll take it,' said the receptionist.

'What's that?'

'You should ride out. Now.'

Balum was surprised. 'Why would you say that?'

'Deputy Cain is out looking for you.'

'Lance Cain?'

'That's the one.'

'How do you know he's looking for me?'

'He came by here this afternoon.'

'What!'

'Said something about you being a thief. He's gunning for you; you should be careful. There's something wrong with that man.'

'Why didn't you tell me he was here?'

'You came in here stumbling drunk. I was too busy avoiding your hands, if you recall.'

'Did he go up to my room?'

'He's the deputy. He goes wherever he wants.'

'Goddammit, Charlise!'

'Watch your tongue, Balum. It's not my fault he was in your room. Whatever trouble you've got brewing between you and the sheriff isn't my affair. And I'm not about to tell that creep Cain what he can and cannot do.'

Balum ran his hand down the length of his face. He let Charlise have the last word and walked out into the street.

Now what? They had his gold. What Charlise had said made sense; he should ride out. While he still could. But Balum already knew he wasn't going to do that. He never could leave well enough alone. The true owner of that gold was dead, buried up in Hell Country in an unmarked grave. Now it was in the hands of his killers. Maybe Balum didn't have the most honest claim to that gold, but he sure as hell deserved it more than the DeLaces.

He drew his gun from its holster and checked the rounds. From here on out he needed to keep his ears to the ground.

9

Inside the Independent, Balum scanned around for the waiter he knew. Not seeing him, he grabbed the shoulder of a bargirl.

'I'd like to know how much credit I've got here. The name's Balum.'

'Yes sir, I'll check.'

She crossed the room and after a quick chat with the barman, returned to Balum. 'You have two dollars credit remaining.'

'Give it to me in cash.'

Two dollars wasn't much, but Balum knew how he could turn it into more. If he was going to stick around in Bette's Creek any longer and get his gold back, he was going to need something to stake him.

He left the Independent and made his way across the street toward the Candelabra. The moon was nearly full, and its reflection lit up the street well enough to make shadows. Lanterns were hung outside all the establishments on Main Street, and light poured through the windows.

Balum looked over to the sheriff's office. All was dark. That meant DeLace and Cain could be anywhere. They might even be in the Candelabra, but that was a risk Balum would need to take.

Crossing through the swinging doors, Balum paused and surveyed the room. Now this was a gambling hall. Tables filled with miners, businessmen, cowpunchers, shopkeepers and travelers crowded the room. Women were plentiful, and all for sale. They flirted with the men, urging them to drink more, each whore acutely aware of where the money was at any moment.

The noise of conversation, the shouts, the groans, it made it seem even larger than it was. A long bar stretched across the entire back wall where two barmen furiously poured drinks.

He made his way through roulette wheels and craps tables, past the baccarat players and blackjack dealers, until he finally came to a stop. The poker tables spread out before him. The gamblers here were slightly quieter than those whom he had just passed. They kept their cards close to their chests or face down on the tables, and eyed each other silently. Some men stood observing, some waiting for a seat to open up.

Balum waited with them, watching the action. Most of the men drank; a few did not. Fortunes were made and lost in an instant here. The game at the table in front of him moved quickly. Six men, each with a pile of coins and bills in front of him.

Balum leaned over to the man standing beside him. 'What's the buy-in?'

'Five dollars at this table. Those,' he motioned further back, 'are ten dollar buy-ins, and the table in the far back is a twenty dollar minimum.'

Balum pinched the coins in his pocket. He needed three more dollars fast. He turned and strolled back through the room and stopped at the roulette table. The croupier had just released the ball onto the spinning wheel, and the men who had placed their bets waited anxiously. It struck black nineteen. The croupier placed the marker, then raked in the losing coins and dealt payouts to the lucky ones.

'Alright folks, place your bets, place your bets!'

Balum took the two dollar coins from his pocket and placed them on the red box at the side of the table. When all had placed their bets, the croupier spun the wheel and dropped the white ball into the chute. The ball raced along the wheel for a few seconds, then began to bounce choppily. It came to a standstill on red, thirty. The croupier stacked two more coins on top of Balum's. Balum kept his hands at his sides. Men placed their bets. The croupier spun the wheel and dropped the ball. Balum could feel his teeth clench together. He bit harder as the ball started to bounce, and when it finally came to a stop on red he let his breath out.

With eight dollars in his pocket he stood waiting at the poker tables. When a seat opened he sat down, put his coins in front of him, and gave a nod in response to the other players' greetings. This group was a talkative bunch, and as they played, they ribbed each other and let loose with the town gossip.

Balum listened while he played, but said nothing. The hands he was getting were weak. His money pile slowly began to shrink. As the men dealt and bet money, the talk invariably turned to the mines. The town was built on the backs of the mines, and their fortunes foretold those of the gamblers.

'Sheriff's mine is paying off, ain't she?' said one.

'Two pounds of nuggets they found, soon as they bought it!' said another. 'Too bad it got stole!'

Balum took up his hand. Another bunch of random cards. He was irritated. 'Is that right they don't actually have a deed to that mine?' he asked.

'Deed got burnt up in that fire,' replied a gambler.

'And the man who owned that claim was never found,' added Balum.

'He got burned up too. Sheriff buried the ashes.'

'Seems strange,' said Balum, folding his hand.

'What are you saying is strange?' asked one of the men.

'Just noting it's odd,' said Balum. 'They say they had two pounds of gold stolen within a few hours of taking possession of that claim. Some of you are miners yourselves. I've tried my hand at it. Can any of you imagine coming up with two pounds in a matter of hours?'

He had their attention now. Game play had stopped and the men standing around the table moved in closer.

'And who was doing the mining in those few hours? It was the sheriff's daughter who was there. Did she mine that gold?'

Folks started murmuring.

Balum felt good. His cards weren't lucky, but he was giving people something to chew on that they hadn't before considered.

Balum continued, 'This time a year ago there wasn't anything to this town. Now it's big, business is moving. We've got gambling, liquor, women. Plenty to take our minds off things. But do any of you know this sheriff? This DeLace? Where'd he come from? Who elected him?'

'You start making that kind of talk without nothing to back it up, mister, and you're looking to get shot,' said a heavily bearded miner with a pile of chips in front of him. 'Now you got some kind of proof, or are you just making talk?'

Balum hesitated. He didn't have any proof. 'Like I said, I'm just noting that it's odd.'

'Let's get on with the game, boys,' said another.

They dealt cards and Balum came up with an ace and a king. It was the best hand he'd had all night. He exchanged his other three and was left with a pair of kings. He raised, and the rest folded except for one. They raised each other back and forth until Balum called. When they showed their cards Balum had been beaten by a set of three tens.

His pile had dwindled back to his two original

dollars. He couldn't keep going much longer. The next hand came around and he was dealt ace high. He had to go with it. His trade-ins didn't give him much, but that was poker. It was a game of bluffs, and it was time to test his. He shoved his two dollars forward and leaned his chair onto its back legs. The man to his left folded. So did the next. Balum held his breath. The next man folded. Two more to go. The next in line waited, watching Balum. He threw in two dollars. Balum swore under his breath. The next man put in two dollars as well, and raised the pot another dollar.

They created a separate pot, and Balum watched, dejected, when they finally showed their cards. Both of the other players had better hands. His last two dollars were raked away into the pile of another man.

Balum got up from the table and walked to the side of the gambling hall and stood with his back leaning against the wall. He didn't even have enough money to buy himself a beer. He was up a creek.

A wild chorus of shouts suddenly went up from the craps table. The whole gambling hall turned to look, curious to know what had just been won. The craps table routinely broke out in shouts, and each time it drew the room's attention.

Balum looked around. He sure wished he had that gold. The fun he could have here was immeasurable. As he looked at the gamblers and the whores, his gaze was arrested by a figure at the bar. A young woman with silky hair stood all the way at one end where the barkeep door could flip open. Balum looked more closely. Why did she seem so familiar? Maybe he was mistaken. Then she turned, and Balum saw her profile. Cynthia!

Now what was she doing here? She wasn't a working girl. In fact, she wore a large coat covering up her sensual body, hiding her enormous breasts from the men's eyes. Balum had hardly recognized her.

He pulled his hat down and watched her out of the corner of his eye. She stood alone, minding her own business and watching the crowd of drunks. She twirled an empty glass in front of her.

Suddenly the craps table erupted again in shouts and hoots. Balum looked in their direction as did everyone else. Immediately he swung his head back toward the bar. Cynthia had already slid through the barkeep door and had her hand in the cash drawer. The barkeeps stood on their tiptoes, looking across the room to the craps table. In an instant she was back around to the other side of the bar and fiddling again with the empty glass.

I'll be damned, thought Balum. I just caught the Candelabra thief.

10

He waited until Cynthia had taken all she was going to steal for the night, and left shortly after she did. Although his hotel was situated just behind the Candelabra, he stepped out warily, keeping to the shadows.

When he opened the door to the hotel, Cynthia was hanging her overcoat on the coat rack. She had placed the wad of stolen cash on the reception counter. Balum's eyes fell on it and she snatched it up, a guilty look on her face.

Balum smiled at her and walked toward the counter. 'Good evening, young lady.'

'Good evening, Mr. Balum,' she stammered, shoving the stack of bills into the register. Her breasts looked extra creamy in the dim light of the reception area. They jiggled when she slammed the register closed.

'Not doing so bad here, huh?'

'Business has been good.'

'Bullshit,' he said, circling around the desk. He came up next to her and leaned an elbow on the counter. She stood with her back to the register, as if defending it. Her arms were crossed behind her, her young breasts shoved out toward Balum.

'What do you mean?' she asked.

'I was in the Candelabra tonight.'

She didn't say anything. Her breath came in quick bursts, and he could feel it on his throat. Her breasts heaved up with each inhalation.

'I think you're much cuter without that big overcoat on though,' he said, and brought his hand up to her smooth cheek. He ran his fingers along her jaw and put his thumb on her bottom lip and pulled it down slightly.

'That sure draws people's attention when they land those big bets on the craps table, don't it.'

'I...I...' she stuttered.

'Sheriff is all worked up about who's been fleecing the Candelabra. Probably because he knows if he doesn't bring some semblance of law and order to this town he'll get run out. He's just itching to find the crook.'

'Oh my God,' whispered Cynthia. 'You're not going to tell him, are you? We'd be in so much trouble.'

'No, I don't think I need to tell him anything at all.'

Cynthia sighed in relief, 'Oh, thank you.'

'...as long as you convince me not to,' said Balum, moving his hand down to the side of her breast and squeezing it in his rough hand.

'What do you want me to do?' asked Cynthia, glancing down at his hand.

'How about you start by showing me these great big titties of yours.'

'If I do, you won't tell the sheriff?'

'Well, that might convince me a little bit,' he smiled.

She slowly reached behind her and untied the ribbons holding her dress up. The top of it fell to her waist, revealing two giant round breasts of creamy skin. She had large pink areolas and small firm nipples. Her breasts were as round as two melons, and stood straight out from her chest without hanging an inch. They were young and firm, and he grabbed them in his hands and squeezed them, burying his face into them and sucking the nipples. They smelled of young fresh skin, recently soaped.

Her head tilted back and she let out a quiet moan as he pinched her hard nipples.

'What else do I have to do?' she asked.

Balum pulled the chair around to him. 'Get on your knees,' he said.

Cynthia dropped to her knees, her breasts bouncing up and down. Balum unbuttoned his trousers and pulled out his hardened dick. He sat in the chair in front of the girl and wagged his cock in front of her.

'Wrap your pretty lips around my dick for me,' he said.

She reached her hand out and gripped the base of

his cock and looked up at him. She brought her mouth to it, looking him innocently in the eye the whole time, and slowly slid its length into her mouth.

Balum let out a sigh as he watched her. He reached down and grabbed one of her tits and bounced it in his palm. It was heavy and soft, all at the same time. Cynthia began to bob her head up and down, slobbering on his cock. She reached her other hand under his balls and gently rolled them in her fingers.

Balum ran his hand through her hair and grabbed a tuft of it close to her skull. He rammed her face onto his cock, feeling the tip of it slam up against the back of her throat. She coughed and gagged, and pulled his shaft out to catch her breath. She looked up at him. Drool dripped down her lips and over her chin. He rubbed the head of his dick over her soft cheeks while she caught her breath.

'Is this how you like it, Mr. Balum?' she whispered.

'That's right, just like that.'

'You won't tell anybody?'

'Your secret's safe with me,' he said, and slid his dick back into her waiting mouth.

He closed his eyes and relaxed in the chair while she sucked away. He listened to her slurping, felt the weight of her titties in his lap.

Suddenly he heard a noise out of place and he opened his eyes. The door behind the reception area opened and Charlise stepped through. She took one step into the small area behind the counter and came up directly behind her daughter.

She gasped and brought her hands up to her mouth.

Cynthia, noting something had occurred, looked up and saw Balum's expression. She turned her face, covered in slobber and cum, and saw her mother standing behind her. One hand still clutched Balum's cock. She stroked it absentmindedly.

'Cynthia!,' her mother shouted. 'What the hell is going on?'

'Now now, lower your voice,' said Balum.

'You better have a good excuse for this, mister,' fumed Charlise.

'Why don't you explain to your mother, Cynthia.'

The girl still held Balum's erection in her small hand. 'I got caught. Mr. Balum saw me at the Candelabra.'

'What? You idiot,' Charlise had lowered her voice, and she spoke in a throaty whisper. 'I told you to be careful.'

'I was, Mommy, I swear! Mr. Balum is the only one who saw me though.'

'Well now you're in trouble. You're going to have to do whatever he wants now. I'm not going to lose my hotel over this.' She had her hands on her hips and looked down at her daughter. 'Go on then, put it back in your mouth.'

The girl stuck her tongue out and ran Balum's cock over it and into her throat. Balum leaned back in the chair again and looked at Charlise. Her face was flushed red. Clearly she was upset.

'So,' Balum said, as Cynthia sucked his dick, 'you knew your daughter was stealing from the Candelabra.'

'Well, I mean...'

'The way I see it, you're both in this together,' said Balum.

'You're not going to say anything though, right?' said Charlise, her face worried.

'Not about Cynthia.' He took the back of her head and shoved his cock deep into her mouth. The girl moaned. 'She's doing a fine job. You're going to have to do a little work too though.'

Charlise's mouth dropped open and her hands went instinctively to her large breasts.

'That's right,' said Balum. 'Let's see those.'

Cynthia stopped sucking on Balum's cock for a moment. She turned around and watched her mom undo the top of her dress and let it fall to her waist. Charlise's breasts poured out, as perfect as her daughter's. Her skin was slightly darker, and her massive breasts seemed slightly fuller, heavier, yet still perky and firm.

Balum motioned for her to come closer. She did, and he reached out and gave her boobs a hard smack with his hand.

'Ow!' she yelped.

He pulled them to his face and bit her nipples. He licked the soft undersides and shoved as much tit into his mouth as he could take.

'Get down here,' he said.

She knelt to her knees beside Cynthia. She knew

just what to do. She took his cock and guided it past her full lips and into her mouth. She looked him in the eye as she sucked it, lifting her breasts up with her forearm and smacking his balls on the tops of her tits.

She took his cock from her mouth then and spit on it, then shoved it back in. She moaned while she sucked him, bouncing up and down and letting her titties shake for him. Balum reached over and grabbed Cynthia's head. He pulled his shaft from Charlise's mouth and stuck it into Cynthia's. He grabbed each girl by the back of the head. He stood up from the chair then, and slid his dick into each mouth, first Cynthia's, then Charlise's. He alternated, watching them take his cock. Their lips were covered in saliva, and strings of cum clung to their chins. Their mouths were open and waiting for him, and he gripped their hair tightly in his hands as he felt his member swell to its limit.

When he felt he couldn't last any longer, he had Charlise take his cock in her hand and stroke it over her and her daughter's face. They moaned, waiting, their mouths open, eager to receive his load. He burst finally, shooting his load of hot cum over their faces. He drenched them completely, shooting it across their foreheads, their noses, onto their hair and into their open mouths. He squeezed the last bit of jizz into Charlise's mouth, and she took it, swallowing the last of his load.

Balum fell back into the chair exhausted. Maybe things weren't so bad after all, he thought, looking at the girls.

They knelt in front of him, wiping cum from their faces and licking it from their lips. It had dribbled down onto their huge boobs and they rubbed it into their skin like fine lotion.

11

Balum woke to a soft knock at his door the following morning. He grabbed the Dragoon and walked gingerly across the wooden floor. The knock sounded again. He opened the door a crack, the gun hanging at his side, and peered through.

It was Cynthia. Balum frowned. Had she come back for more? He started to speak but she hushed him quickly.

'The sheriff is downstairs. He's putting up warrants for your arrest. They have your picture on them!' she whispered.

He nodded and closed the door. Quickly, he put on his pants and boots, then threw his shirt on. He wasn't sure what to do. He sure as hell didn't want to be arrested. Now that the sheriff had found the gold, he surely suspected Balum knew about Bennett's death and the stolen claim. DeLace would never let that information out. If he was arrested he would hang.

On the other hand, he didn't doubt for a moment

that DeLace would shoot him down if no one was looking. After all, the sheriff was a thief and a murderer. Balum was quick with a gun, but DeLace had Cain along with him. Balum wasn't quick enough for two.

As he stood in his room deliberating on what to do, he thought he heard footsteps on the stairs. He froze, listening. They became louder.

Balum couldn't think quickly enough. Should he surrender or shoot it out? His dragoon lay on the bed where he had thrown it. Before he could reach to pick it up, the door smashed open. Lance Cain's boot came back down to the floor.

'Got you now, boy,' he said, and his hand dropped for his gun.

Balum had no time. He whirled and threw himself into the window, arms crossed over his face. The glass shattered and Balum fell from the second story onto the ground in the alley below. He landed with a whump, the wind briefly knocked from his lungs. He struggled to pick himself up. He had landed on his hip and he limped as he ran toward Main Street.

He heard his name shouted behind him. He looked back and saw Henry DeLace rounding the corner of the hotel and coming down the alley.

Balum ran. He was almost to Main Street. He looked back again, and this time saw the sheriff drawing his gun. Balum ran, but he had been slowed by the fall. His leg gave out and DeLace's gun boomed behind him, missing him by inches.

Balum reached Main Street and threw himself forward. The shot had startled people, and as he came diving through the alley, people stopped what they were doing and stared.

He lay in the street on his back. 'I'm unarmed!' he shouted, as the sheriff came out of the alley, gun drawn.

'I'm unarmed,' he shouted again, his hands in the air.

The sheriff looked about and saw the townsfolk gathered there. Lance Cain was just coming out from the alley.

'It's a good thing you are, Balum,' said the sheriff, and sent his boot into Balum's ribs.

The kick sent Balum sprawling. He rolled over onto his belly and slowly brought himself to all fours. DeLace came in again then, striking him in the stomach with his boot. Balum crumpled, clutching his midsection.

'There he is folks,' said DeLace. 'Take a good look at him.' He turned to the hitch post next to him. On it was tacked a wanted poster with Balum's face on it. The sheriff tore it off and held it up to the crowd. 'One less thief we're going to have to deal with in Bette's Creek,' he shouted at them. He threw the wanted poster down at Balum.

Balum looked at a shaky resemblance of himself. Beneath the portrait were the words *Gold Thief*.

DeLace and Cain grabbed him up by his arms and dragged him across the street to the jail. They shoved him in a cell and closed the bars.

'You should have kept your mouth shut, Balum,' said DeLace. 'Maybe you could have gotten out of here with your pecker still working. But you had to go start talking all over town. I don't like folks talking about me, Balum. I don't like people questioning me, not one bit. Now you reap the consequences.' He turned to his deputy. 'Come on, let's get going.'

'Hope your belly's full, Balum,' sneered Cain. 'Town funds aren't going to be able to feed you nothing.'

He laughed at this, revealing his sickening yellow teeth. DeLace hung the cell keys on the wall and the two left, locking the door behind them. The town would be buzzing and the two wanted all the accolades they could soak up.

Balum watched them leave through the cell bars. When the door shut, nothing but silence remained in the small jail.

It was an old jail, an old cell. Chester had talked about the town being several decades old. All these buildings had been built long ago, many of them empty by the time the gold boom started.

This was one of those buildings.

Balum carefully inspected his cell. An old cot with a tattered blanket, a piss bucket in the corner. The floor was dirt, the walls made of wood planks. The window was small and had two metal bars driven through it.

He felt along the wall, his fingers pressing and pulling at the planks. The jail was old, but it had been built solid. Nothing like those chintzy walls in Charlise's place. He kicked at the wall and came up with nothing but a sore heel.

Then something occurred to him; he'd dig his way out. He dropped to the floor and put his hands to the ground. It was hard clay, similar to some of the earth out in Hell Country. He kicked the toe of his boot into the ground, and after several minutes had only made a small indentation.

He sat back down on the cot and looked at the sky out the window. He had to get out of there. He knew no one here in Bette's Creek. Or did he?

He knew Chester, but Chester was an old man, and despite some friendly words, not liable to break him out of jail.

There was Charlise, and Cynthia. Cynthia had even come to warn him about the sheriff. They sure had enjoyed last night, he thought. But Balum knew it was far-fetched.

That was it. There was no one else. He hung his head and closed his eyes. He'd come a long way to die at the end of a rope.

12

Henry DeLace came back that evening to lock up the jail for the night. He had been out all day accepting the congratulations of the townsfolk.

With him came Deborah. She walked right up to Balum's cell and looked at him. She wore a long dress and a petite overcoat with her hair pulled back. She was strikingly beautiful, her body slim and strong.

She turned to her father. 'I don't want him talking to anybody.'

'He won't be.'

'He knows too much.'

'You're just nervous, Deborah. There's no one in here for him to talk with.'

'He knows everything! He's been running his mouth...why, if he starts talking--'

'I said he won't be. Now let's get going.'

'I want him dead, Daddy.' She turned to look at Balum. Her eyes tore into him. 'This is what happens to foul men who forget to treat a lady with respect.'

She followed her father through the door and it

slammed shut behind them.

Balum let his breath out. What a piece of work! She wanted him dead alright. She knew that the deed to the claim was still out there somewhere. They had told the whole town that Bennett had signed it over to her, and that it had burned up. If that deed came out in the open, with only Bennett's name on it, her and her father would be ousted as killers and thieves. So of course she wanted him dead.

She also wanted him dead out of spite. There was a true dislike she had for him ever since he had insulted her in the gold buyer's shack. She simply wanted to see him suffer.

That irked Balum. That girl thought the world of herself, and for no good reason. She had a beautiful face and a body that would make a man stop and stare, and because of this she thought the world owed her something.

That night the temperature dropped. Balum shivered on his cot. He rubbed his arms with his hands and looked out the window at the stars. He thought back to the last time he had looked up at them. Back in Hell Country. Only a few nights ago, really. His fortunes sure had changed.

With the rising sun the temperature began to creep back up, and Balum finally fell into a slumber. A brief sleep, for only a couple hours later the sheriff opened the jail.

He didn't speak to Balum. He sat at his desk and went over some paperwork as if he were alone. It wasn't long until Cain showed up. He walked right up to Balum's cell and put a hand up to the bars.

'Hear that sound, boy?' he asked, showing off his stained teeth.

Balum listened and heard the normal sounds of the town. Horses, wagons, people moving about.

'You hear the sound of that hammer? That's special, just for you.'

Balum listened again. This time he heard the far off thwack of a hammer hitting wood. He looked at Cain, wondering what the man was driving at.

'What, you don't know?' Cain looked over at DeLace sitting at his desk. 'You ain't told him?'

The sheriff looked up at Cain, then went back to his papers.

Cain turned back to the cell. 'We're building something special for you. Big gallows, edge of town. Going to have your big show on Saturday. Folks all over this here country going to travel out just to see you swinging on that rope. I'll be a little sore to see it myself. I would have liked to have it out with you. You always wore that gun of yours tied down low like you was some kind of quick draw. I'd have filled you full of holes.'

Balum only halfway listened to Cain's bluster. The sound of the hammer seemed to rise above all other sounds of the town. With each blow he imagined the beams rising up, the platform being constructed solely for his death.

The two of them did not stay long. Neither actually

liked work much, preferring instead to amble about the town.

Alone inside the cell, Balum was left with no choice but to listen to the sounds of his gallows being constructed. It was a Thursday. Day after tomorrow he would hang.

He stood up from his cot and in a rage gripped the bars in the window. He shook them furiously, but they wouldn't budge. His ribs still ached from the kicking he had been given, and his hip was sore from the fall. He looked across the room to the keys hanging on the wall. He looked up, but the ceiling offered no means of escape.

That afternoon he heard arguing in front of the jail. He could make out the sheriff's loud voice interspersed with another. The door finally opened and Henry DeLace walked through. Chester followed behind with a cloth-covered plate and Balum's hat.

'You've got five minutes, then I want you out of here,' the sheriff growled.

Chester came up to the cell bars and slid the plate through sideways. The contents fell lopsided against the cloth and Balum quickly flipped the plate horizontally again. He pulled off the cloth. On the plate was a pile of pulled brisket and a buttered slice of cornbread. He nearly felt tears come to his eyes.

The old livery man leaned against the bars. 'Don't have no tableware for you. Brought you your hat. Seems to me a man shouldn't go without his hat no matter where he is.'

He passed it through the cell and Balum took it, shaking his head. 'Chester, I don't know if any plate of food has cheered me up as much as this is doing right now.'

'I wish there was more I could do.'

'You can take good care of the roan for me. He's treated me well. He gets cantankerous every now and then if you push him hard on an empty belly, but he's smart and he's a worker. He's yours now.'

'Thank you, Balum. You ain't got no family I could send for?'

'Got some kin back East. Haven't seen them since I was a boy.'

Chester shook his head. The sheriff sat at his desk watching them.

'I like you, Balum. Sorry to see you on the wrong side of those bars.'

The sheriff stood up, 'Alright, old man, time's up. Take that plate with you; I don't want this bum fiddling with things he shouldn't have.'

When they had left, Balum sat on the cot and listened to the silence. Not that there was no noise coming in from the window; just the hammering had stopped. The sound of the construction progressing along had tormented Balum all day, and now with a belly full of food he relaxed just a touch.

He pulled his legs up and stretched out. This wasn't his last night on earth, he thought, trying to console himself. Anything might happen.

He told himself this, but he didn't much believe it.

13

Another cold and restless night. More strange dreams assaulted him throughout his sleep. He woke early. Dawn slowly brought light into the empty jail. He looked longingly at the key ring hung across the room. His freedom was so close, but there was no way he could see to get it.

DeLace and Cain rambled in by midmorning. Cain dug in at Balum again, eager to see the man's discomfort. He kept Balum apprised of the construction on the end of town.

'She's coming right along. They'll have her built before sundown today. Nice looking gallows they are, all new. And just for you!' he laughed.

The sheriff had sat down to clean his weapons. 'Lance,' he said. 'If you ain't got nothing better to do, then go down to the Candelabra and see if they're still coming up short. I'm not going to listen to this shit all morning.'

Lance left, not hiding his displeasure at all.

Balum could guess why the sheriff didn't want

anyone hanging around. His daughter's worrying was probably rubbing off on him. If Balum did know anything about where that deed was, or if he could produce it, he could turn that Saturday hanging right on its head. The sheriff just might be worrying that Balum would turn up with something in front of the crowd Saturday. Why risk letting him out in front of folks and giving him the opportunity to talk?

He wished he had taken the deed when he grabbed that gold. At least he would have a chip in his pocket. As it stood, no one might see that small bag resting under a rock ledge for years to come.

He didn't see how he had any more bargaining chips. He knew how the Candelabra was coming up short. But Cynthia and Charlise had done more than their fair share to earn his silence. He smiled remembering that night. Besides, he couldn't see how giving them up would do much for him.

Balum watched the sheriff take his weapons apart and lay the pieces over his desk. He wondered if one was meant for him. As he considered the possibility of DeLace shooting him before he had a chance to hang, the jail door opened and in walked Deborah.

Balum leaned forward, worried. The girl threw him an unpleasant look and turned to her father's desk.

'I just heard that old man from the livery was here last night. Is that true?'

'What difference does it make?'

'I told you no visitors!' She stamped her foot. Her anger caused her voice to pinch, and it came out through her nose. It sounded like nearly everything she said came out as a moan.

'It was five minutes, nothing happened.'

'We don't know how much he knows,' she replied hoarsely. 'What if he has it?'

The two of them looked at Balum. He sat silently, playing dumb.

'He ain't got nothing,' said the sheriff. 'We looked through his kit. Didn't have much. Sure didn't have what we need.'

'I don't like it. There's so many people coming into town. What if he knows something? What if he starts talking? They'll listen to him. Everybody listens to what the condemned say before they hang!'

'Goddammit Deborah, I can't think with all of this,' he shouted. 'He's not gonna talk. If he knew anything he already would have said it.'

'We should kill him, Daddy. Kill him right now!'

'Stop it! Lower your damn voice. He's hanging tomorrow and this will be over. Now get out of here and give me some peace.'

She looked at Balum one more time, her face furious.

Balum's heart pounded. He felt nauseous. That girl would kill him right then if she had the means. Balum was glad that all the weapons in the room were currently in pieces getting cleaned.

When she left he was no more at ease than before. Henry DeLace finished his cleaning and began to reassemble the arms. Balum could only hope the girl's words weren't affecting her father.

When DeLace finally did pick up his coat and leave, Balum took several long breaths. He shook his head. What was the point of getting shaken up at the idea of dying one day earlier? Still, it didn't seem real that tomorrow he would hang. He stood in the small cell for quite some time, as if in a trance.

Before he knew it, night had fallen. Neither the sheriff nor the deputy had come back. That was fine with Balum. The jail grew darker until the only light was that which came through the windows. The moon was full, and its light was like a faraway streetlamp.

He could hear noises outside. Hoof falls, wagon wheels, the clink of glasses. Then he heard something else; the jail door squeaking on its hinges.

It opened fast and a figure stepped through, shutting it just as quickly. Balum squinted in the dark. He heard the footfalls and recognized them instantly; Deborah!

She walked up to his cell. He stepped back against the wall.

'You're not going to get in my way, you bastard,' she said, and drew a revolver from her handbag.

Balum threw his hands up. 'Whoa whoa whoa,' he stammered. He might have expected a small derringer, but she had pulled out an old Colt Walker revolver with a nine inch barrel and had it pointed directly at his chest.

14

'Easy now,' he scrambled for words. 'You shoot me now and you'll be doing your own self in.'

'What do you mean by that?' she hesitated.

'You want that claim deed, I can give it to you.'

'You have it?'

'I can get it.'

'Don't think I won't shoot you. I'll do anything for that deed.' She cocked the hammer back. 'Where is it?'

She might miss once or twice, as unlikely as that was, but that Colt Walker held six rounds and she wasn't going to miss six times. Not with him stuck in that shooting gallery.

'A short ride from here,' he answered.

'Tell me right now or I'll shoot you.'

'If I do, you'll sure as hell shoot me. I know you're worried I'll go screaming its whereabouts to the whole county before I hang.'

'Exactly. So I'll shoot you right now.'

'Won't do you any good. It's plain out in the open. I'm surprised no one has found it by now,' he lied.

Deborah held the gun straight out with her arm extended. That weapon weighed nearly five pounds and she was feeling it. 'How do I know you're telling the truth?'

'That deed belonged to Doug Bennett. Witnessed by two Recorders at the County Records Office. He signed for it in March of last year.'

'Where is it?'

'Put that gun down. You want that deed, let me go get it.'

'I don't trust you,' she whined through her nose.

'You can shoot me now or let me hang tomorrow, but either way that deed is going to be in someone's hands soon, and it won't be your hands. Your story of it burning will be seen as a lie and you'll be run out of town or worse. Your only chance is with me.'

She stood looking at him, the gun hanging heavy in her hand.

'How far away is it?'

'A few hour's ride.'

She stared at him intently. He could make out her face in the faint moonlight. As ornery as she was, she was still a beauty. Finally she turned and took the keys from the wall. She came back to the cell.

'I'm going to unlock the cell. You'll come out and walk in front of me. My horse is tied outside. I'll untie him, and you'll walk in front of me to the livery stable. You'll get your horse there and we'll ride out. I'll be holding my gun inside my handbag with my finger on the trigger. If you attract any attention or make any move I don't like I'll shoot you dead in the back and when you fall I'll shoot you again through the back of your head. You understand?'

'Jesus,' said Balum.

'And don't take the Lord's name in vain or I'll shoot you for that.'

'Alright. I'll move careful. Don't shoot me before you get that deed in your hands.'

She walked behind him just like she said she would. He didn't need to turn around to know that the old Colt Walker was aimed right at his backside.

The few people in the street took no notice of them. They reached the livery and drew the slide bar from its resting place without anyone taking a second look. Balum threw his saddle blanket over the roan and cinched the saddle over top. They rode out then, neither one exchanging a word with the other.

The moon was bright. It shone its light down on them and cast shadows of their horses onto the dirt. Deborah, still distrustful of him, let him take the lead.

Balum rode at a trot. He could hear Deborah's horse behind him. He knew she'd have that gun pointed right at his back, and he felt no desire to turn around to verify this. His mind needed to work quickly. Balum generally liked to look at a problem from a few angles and spend time picking away at it until he found a solution he was satisfied with. Tonight was about thinking fast though.

He rode as if he knew exactly where he was going. He sat tall in his saddle and took in his surroundings. Truth was though, he couldn't exactly recall where that rock slab was located. It had been daylight when he had passed through here, and he had been riding in the opposite direction. Now all of Hell Country was lit up under the light of the moon. It played tricks on the eyes.

What would Deborah do after she got the deed? Shoot him? What if he couldn't find it? Well she'd sure as hell shoot him then. Balum's eyes fogged up as he thought it over. She had already said she'd do anything for that deed.

He thought back to the jail, and how worked up she had been when speaking with her father. He considered her actions tonight. She just broke him out of jail! It occurred to Balum then that the girl might have lost her mind. She had killed a man, stolen his claim, but hadn't tied things off correctly. The idea of that deed winding up in someone's hands was too much for her.

He slowed his horse to a walk. A dry arroyo was coming up and he remembered crossing one shortly after grabbing the gold. They crossed it and he let his horse begin to zig-zag in long stretches.

After a few cutbacks Deborah spoke up behind him. 'What's all this turning?' she whined.

'We're close now. Don't want to pass it up.'

'You said it was right out in the open. We're in the

middle of nowhere.'

'It is. You'll see,' he stalled.

They rode on a bit more. The cold was settling in, and he wished he had his overcoat. He looked back. The girl rode with her free hand clutching her jacket tight to her body.

Ahead he could see piles of rock and upthrusts of stone. He was close.

'How much longer is this going to take?' Deborah started up again. 'It's cold out here.'

'Not much longer.'

'I want that deed.'

She wanted it alright. She had lost her mind over it, thought Balum. He rode up next to an outcropping and drew his horse up. He recognized this place. He had lain down behind these same rocks when the posse rode through.

'You'll get it,' Balum said, and dismounted.

15

Deborah looked around, her face angry. 'Where are we?'

'Your deed is right over yonder. Fifty yards. Couple minutes of hunting and I'll have it.'

'Go hunt then,' she whined.

Balum stood and looked up at her sitting on her horse.

'Well? What are you waiting for? Go find it. Find it or I'll shoot you.'

'Naw,' said Balum. 'I don't think you will.'

'What?' She held the gun at him, her face shocked. 'Of course I will!'

'I've been doing some thinking. You need that deed. Shoot me before you get it and you'll never find peace. You'll live the rest of your life looking over your shoulder, wondering when someone is going to walk into town with the deed to the claim you stole. You say you'll shoot me. You won't though. Not before I hand it to you, anyway.'

He rested his hand on his saddle horn while he

spoke, watching her all the while. She said nothing, only staring at him with that ornery look stuck on her face.

'Now after I give it to you, that's when it gets tricky,' he continued, walking over to her horse. 'After that you sure won't want me around. I'm the last one who knows things aren't on the level. I have no doubt you'll shoot me then.'

'What do you propose?'

'You've already said you'll do anything for that deed,' said Balum. He stood right next to her.

'So?'

'So if I'm going to be a dead man in a few minutes I'd at least like to see just what it is you're willing to do for it.' He put a hand on her thigh.

'I knew you were an animal.'

'Well this animal wants some fun before he dies. Now get off your horse.'

She dismounted and stood in front of him, the gun held at her waist, the barrel pointed at Balum's gut.

'You might be an ornery bitch, but you're a damn pretty one,' he said, and reached a hand into her jacket and felt one of her tits through her dress. 'Take that jacket off.'

'It's cold,' she complained.

'You'll get warm quick.'

She took the jacket off, switching the gun from one hand to the other. Once off, he drove his hand down the front of her dress and under her brassiere, fondling her tits. They were firm, just under a handful.

His dick hardened and he unbuttoned his trousers and took it out. Deborah looked down at it and frowned.

'Take my cock in your hand and stroke it,' he told her.

As she did so he leaned closer, putting a hand behind her head and kissing her mouth. As close as they were, the barrel of the gun sunk slightly into his midsection.

'You better not be lying to me about that deed,' said Deborah, pulling her mouth from his and running her hand up and down his shaft.

'You'll get it. You're going to earn it though. Take that dress off.'

She slipped the dress from her shoulders and let it fall to the ground.

'Take the rest off.'

She stripped off the brassiere and panties and stood naked in front of him. The moonlight reflected off her body, revealing two beautiful young breasts, a flat stomach and small waist. Her hips widened and below were two strong thighs, smooth and light.

He reached a hand between them and spread her pussy lips apart with his fingers. He let one graze the inside of her cunt, feeling its wetness on his finger.

'You find what you want?' she whined, looking up at him.

'Lay down.'

The red clay of the desert floor still held some warmth from the day's sunlight. Deborah reclined onto her back and Balum knelt between her legs. He grabbed her thighs in both hands and lifted her legs, spreading them apart. He could smell the scent of her sex.

She reached forward and grabbed his cock with her hand, the other still holding the gun. 'You only get a little bit. Then I want the deed.' She guided his cock up to her cunt, and pressed the tip of it against her wet lips. 'Only put the tip in,' she said. 'My pussy is small and your cock is too big for it.'

Balum couldn't stand it anymore. With one thrust he rammed his cock deep inside her, up to the hilt.

Deborah let out a cry through her nose. It carried through the thin desert air, a nasally moan drifting out into the dark.

Balum slammed his cock into her again and again as she moaned out. He grabbed her tits and leaned his face in to bite her nipples, lick her neck, devour her.

He gripped her by the hip and flipped her over suddenly. She knelt on her knees, her head resting on her forearms. Balum placed both hands around her small waist and shoved his dick into her. She was soaking wet now, and he could hear his cock plumbing her pussy even over the sound of her constant moaning.

As he looked down at her perfect ass he took a finger and began to play with her asshole. When he stuck a finger inside she yelped and turned her face around in surprise.

'Oh my God, what do you think you're doing?'

'You said you'd do anything,' said Balum, and withdrew his cock from her pussy. He then placed the tip on her asshole and with one hand under her belly and the other grabbing his shaft, he pushed his dick slowly into her butt.

'Ahhh,' she cried.

He began to pump, slowly at first, then faster, and with each hump she would let out a yelp. He gripped her by her narrow waist and fucked her tight asshole until finally he could hold out no longer. He felt his dick swell, and shot his cum into her ass, pressing her soft cheeks into his hips.

'Oh my God!' she cried out. 'Please, put it back in my pussy. Please,' she whimpered.

Balum's cock was still rigid. He slid it back into her moist vagina. She reached underneath her body and rubbed her clitoris with her spare hand. His cum began to slowly drip out of her ass, glistening in the moonlight. Almost immediately she orgasmed, sending an extended wail out into the night.

She was still stretched out on her knees, face down on the arm that held the gun. While she continued to rub her cunt in pleasure, Balum reached forward and grabbed the gun from her hand.

He stood. She rolled onto her side, her mouth open, one hand massaging her pussy. He tucked his cock back into his trousers and took a step back.

'You bastard,' she whispered. 'Are you going to give me that deed now?'

He walked over to where the rock slab covered the

bag. He picked it up and carried it back to her.

'You earned it,' he said, tossing her the bag. He looked at the Colt Walker in his hand. He needed a gun badly, but not this one. It would do no good carrying this girl's gun around.

'I'm going to leave this gun on the ground over thataway,' he pointed. 'You're going to head back to town and I'm riding into Hell Country. You're not going to follow me.'

He put a foot into his stirrup and swung into the saddle. He took one more look at her as she pulled on her panties, then he turned and rode away.

16

Back into Hell Country he rode, his mind still churning. The night was growing colder, and without a coat he couldn't keep riding like this. As he entered more broken country he pulled up next to a wall of sandstone and unsaddled his horse. He lied down in the sand and covered himself with the blanket and the saddle and closed his eyes.

When he woke the sun had come up. He had no water, no food, and no gun. Not even a plug of tobacco. But as he sat in the morning sun he realized that he did in fact have a plan.

The deed he had given to Deborah was only useful to her in the sense that no one else could find it. The townsfolk were under the impression that it had burned in the fire. Producing it now would only show that she and her father had lied. She had most likely already destroyed it, thought Balum.

There was something else though. They had told the town that Bennett's body had also burned in the fire. But Balum knew exactly where it was buried. Well, he thought, not exactly where. But with a little searching he was sure he could come up with it. If he rode into town with that bullet-ridden body across his horse, that would be the end of the DeLaces.

He stood up and saddled his horse. He could ride until around noon. By then it would be too hot to go on without water. How far away was that body buried? His mind went back to those days he spent crossing Hell Country. After he had come upon the digger he had followed him for only a few hours before making camp. The next day he had caught up with him within just a couple hours, and not long after that the posse showed up.

That meant the body was not all that far off. Maybe a six hour ride.

He started off at a good trot. It didn't take long for the sun to start heating things up, and he slowed to a walk. The sun hit the red clay earth and bounced its heat back up at him. He plodded along and watched the horizon turn to shimmers.

Not much lived out there. Cacti didn't even grow, it was so dry. He looked to the sky and saw no buzzards. They didn't even bother there. Nothing died where nothing lived.

He looked backwards from time to time to check his backtrail. There wasn't any way to conceal his tracks. If a posse had been assembled it wouldn't be hard to follow him.

He pushed on and the sun beat down harder. The

roan began to slow its pace. Sweat ran down his brow and into his eyes. It soaked his shirt, wetting it front and back. He looked for shade, and after another stretch of riding he came upon a short ridge. Descending to the other side he discovered that a section of it was carved out a few feet deep. He dismounted and led the horse into the shade.

Immediately, the difference in temperature was apparent. He sat down and took his hat off. From his small bit of shelter he watched the red desert bake in the sunlight. Oases appeared and disappeared. Occasionally a dust devil would pop up and race along the sand.

As he watched the scene before him he realized that he was scheduled to hang by the neck that very day. They had built gallows just for him. People had even traveled in from the surrounding countryside to make a picnic of it. He wondered what they were all doing now.

He swallowed. His mouth was dry. He picked a pebble out of the dust and rubbed it clean then put it in his mouth. He let it rest under his tongue. An old indian trick someone had taught him years back.

After some time had gone by, he stepped out and measured his shadow. When it grew as long as he was tall, he saddled up and rode on. His horse didn't much like it, but they both knew there wasn't anything else to do but keep on moving.

He scanned the country as he rode. He knew what he was looking for; a hundred foot tall ridge that dropped down steeply. How many such ridges were there in Hell Country? He wasn't sure. If he got too far off track he might never see it. As it was, this country was hilly and broken and jagged. Being off by more than a mile might keep him from spotting the cliff.

As he considered this he saw what might be a ridge some distance to the south. At least a mile. It was hard to believe he had drifted that far north. Time was moving quickly. If he gambled on that ridge and was wrong, his situation would get much more difficult, and fast.

He turned south anyway. He crossed a couple dry arroyos and had to dismount to walk his horse slowly over some jagged rock. Once he neared the ridge he knew he had found his place. Riding along its base he came up to the unmarked grave just as the sun was setting.

He hopped off the saddle and set to digging. He pulled away the rocks and swept the sand and clay away with his forearms. Quickly he was sweating, his heart pounding in his chest. Once he had uncovered the man's shirt he grabbed the front of it and pulled the deadman from the grave. The smell made Balum drop the body and back up. His horse whinnied and stomped off a few feet to one side.

Balum looked at the roan. 'Better get used to it,' he said. 'He's coming with us.'

The dry air of the desert had preserved the man fairly well. Rigor mortis had set in and he was stiff as a board, but his face would be clearly recognizable to anyone who saw it.

Balum was worn out, but he knew he had to get back to Bette's Creek tonight. The sheriff wouldn't let him escape like he had. He'd send a posse, and that posse would surely find him tomorrow.

The sun had set, and Balum had a long ride ahead of him on a tired and thirsty horse. Gathering his strength, he threw the corpse over the back of the horse behind the saddle. As stiff as the body was, there was no way to tie the hands and feet under the horse's belly. There wasn't much Balum could do, so he climbed into the saddle and reached an arm behind him to steady the corpse's legs, which stuck straight out to the side.

It was going to be a long ride back to Bette's Creek.

They moved slowly. No water in that desert sapped one's strength, whether human or horse. The air being as dry as it was seemed to suck water out of a man even in the cold of night. And cold it was. As they rode the temperature dropped. The heat driven into the desert floor throughout the day was released back into the clear night sky.

Balum rubbed his arms while at the same time gripping the deadman's legs. If Bennett had been wearing a coat, Balum would have put it on in spite of the stench. All he could do though was rub his arms and legs and shiver. He was dog tired but there was no hope of dozing off in the saddle in that kind of cold.

The moon and stars made their way across the sky, marking the passage of time. He didn't stop to rest or to give his horse a breather. He needed to make it back to town before sunup. The first thing he needed to do was track down his gun. He wouldn't mind some food in his belly either, but Balum didn't count on that happening all too soon.

As for what he would do once the townsfolk had seen Bennett's body, he wasn't too sure. He'd need to be on the lookout for Henry DeLace. And there was no telling how that harebrained deputy would react, either. This was certainly a play your cards as you go situation, thought Balum.

Either way, it was get the gun back, get the gold back.

In that order.

17

When Bette's Creek finally appeared, still and quiet on the desert floor, the sun was threatening to rise in the east.

It was still early enough to beat the early risers. Balum rode directly to the livery stable on the edge of town. He took down the slide bar and led his horse inside. Chester was nowhere around. The old man would know something was wrong just from the smell of the place; Bennett's body was getting riper by the hour. With no easy solution at hand, Balum untied the corpse and dragged it into an empty stall. He threw a bit of hay over top and stood back to take a look. That wouldn't do for more than a few minutes. It was all Balum could think to do though. He needed to make it to Charlise's place, get his gun, and get back to the livery before anyone could spot him.

He quickly unsaddled his horse and put him back in his stall. He rubbed him down quickly and scooped up a half bucket of oats from the bin. The roan had its head stuck in the watering trough, and Balum nearly put his own face in as well. As sorely as he needed a drink right now, he had to get moving.

He stepped outside. Dusk was breaking. He walked around the side of the building to get off the main drag. He followed the side street along up to Charlise's, pausing at each corner, his hat pulled low over his brow.

Stepping through the door, the reception area was dark and empty. He walked to the back of the desk to see if his belongings had been stashed somewhere but he came up with nothing.

He picked up the small bell from the desk and jingled it. He waited, conscious of every passing second. Finally the door behind the reception area opened and Charlise came through. When she saw Balum she nearly jumped. For that matter, so did Balum.

Charlise had wrapped her robe loosely around her body. No one ever needed attention at this hour of the morning. She half expected the ring to be a false alarm, and had hardly bothered to cover herself.

The robe was made of a thin material. The way she wore it, the ends barely crossed in front, allowed her enormous breasts to stretch the material tight. Her cleavage showed half of the tits themselves, and Balum found himself short of words.

'Balum! What are you doing here?'

'I need my gun, Charlise. The rest of my kit I can leave here, but I need my gun bad.'

'Don't you know there's a posse out looking for you?'

'I figured as much.'

'The whole town is talking about you. People came from fifty miles away to watch you hang. DeLace put the word out for everyone to stay. He promised he'd have you hung by Sunday. That's today!' Charlise exclaimed. 'How did you break out of jail? The whole town is talking about it.'

'That's a long story Charlise. I'll tell it to you another time. Now tell me you haven't gone and sold my gun off.'

'No, I have it.'

'Good.'

'I don't know if I should give it to you though. I don't want to get myself wrapped up in this. They say you're the one who stole the DeLace's gold.'

'That's a lie Charlise. It's the DeLaces who stole that gold, and they killed Bennett for it.'

'Even if that's true, no one is going to believe it. You don't have any proof.'

'I do now. They said Bennett died in the fire and they buried him. Well guess what. I've got Bennett's body filled with holes, sitting in the livery right now.'

Charlise was incredulous. She rubbed her eyes, as if finally waking up. 'Are you serious?'

'Damn right I am. Now get me my gun before some fool sees me and shoots me for a bounty. I'm about to show this town who their sheriff really is.'

'Okay, I'll get it. Let me get dressed first, I want to

see this.'

Charlise disappeared behind the door. Balum waited impatiently. He could feel the lack of sleep catching up to him. When she returned she was dressed in her usual getup, less revealing than the robe but still far from modest.

She carried with her Balum's gun belt and Dragoon revolver. Balum slung it around his hips and checked the rounds in the chamber. A wave of relief hit him. He had felt vulnerable without his gun. Feeling the weight riding on his hips again gave him his confidence back.

They made their way down the backstreet to the livery. People were up now, and had started to go about their business. Balum was glad Charlise was with him; with her half-hanging out of her dress like she was, no one paid him any mind.

When they arrived at the livery the doors were swung open. They could hear Chester inside, cursing to himself.

He stood in front of the stall where Balum had stashed Bennett's body. His head swung towards Balum and Charlise, his eyes so wide you could see the whites on top and bottom.

'Balum!' he shouted.

'Quiet,' said Balum his hand raised up. 'Sorry I wasn't able to warn you about this.'

'What the hell is going on? That's Doug Bennett laying dead in my stable!'

'That's right it is. Burned in a fire, my ass.'

'Where'd you find him?'

'Hell Country.'

Charlise had craned her neck into the stable and when she saw the decomposing body she gagged and covered her nose and mouth. 'Oh my Lord, that's poor Doug Bennett.'

'I told you I wasn't lying,' said Balum.

'What are you going to do now?' asked Charlise.

Balum looked around the livery stable. A small wagon with the sides rotting off sat at one end. 'Let me borrow that wagon.'

'Don't work too good.'

'I won't need it for long.'

Balum led his horse out of the stall and led him back to the wagon. Chester helped get the harness and gear on and they hitched up the wagon. They loaded the stinking corpse onto the back of it, and Balum took the reins of his horse and led it outside.

It was full morning now. The town had woken up. Shops were open and the streets were filling up. Balum walked his horse down the center of Main Street. At the other end stood the newly built gallows, reaching twenty feet into the air. The sight of them made his stomach drop. A good number of wagons surrounded them. These would belong to out of towners, reserving the choicest spots. He stopped his horse in front of the Candelabra.

People had started to notice something was happening. The nosier ones approached the wagon to get a look at the deadman. It didn't take long for someone to recognize who it was.

'It's Doug Bennett!' one of them shouted.

They came in now, crowding around. Word spread down the street like locusts decimating a wheat field. People poured out of saloons, restaurants, hotels and barbershops and everywhere else. Soon there were over fifty people crowded around the wagon.

While they shouted and gossiped and held their noses, Balum climbed into the wagon alongside the body and held his arms up.

'Listen up folks,' he boomed. Their heads came up and they lowered their chattering. 'I'm the man who was scheduled to hang from those yesterday,' he pointed to the gallows.

'You the man they call Balum?' shouted one of the on-lookers.

'That's right. Your sheriff has told you all that I'm a thief, and that I stole his gold. He maintains that he and his daughter mined that gold after they bought it from Doug Bennett. They also say Bennett burned up along with the deed to the claim. Well here's Doug Bennett's body, shot full of holes. Deborah DeLace shot him, and Sheriff DeLace helped steal that gold and hide the body. The only thieves here are Henry and Deborah DeLace. Thieves, and murderers as well!'

The crowd erupted again into chatter. Balum hushed them and continued on. 'A lot of you have come in from around the countryside to see a hanging. Well don't go anywhere just yet. You'll get your hanging.'

The hum of conversation grew again, and Balum looked out over the crowd. As he did, he saw someone approaching from down the street. Something about the man arrested his attention. He focused his eyes.

It was Deputy Cain.

18

He came walking down the street slow-like, his head tilted to the side and a strange grimace on his face. Word had reached him that Bennett's body was sitting on Main Street. When he came outside, Balum's words had carried a good distance. Cain heard DeLace being called out as a thief and a murderer, and something snapped in his head.

Balum climbed down from the wagon, eyeing Cain over the top of the crowd. The look on Balum's face gave something away, and the crowd that had gathered followed his gaze. When they began to realize what was happening the people quickly disappeared from the street, and instead lined up against the rows of buildings. They had come to Bette's Creek for excitement, and they'd found it.

Balum stepped away from the wagon and watched Cain. He'd just come through Hell Country with no sleep, no food, and no water, but right then his senses were sharp. He felt no nervousness. He felt calm, time slowed momentarily. The sounds of the street disappeared. He only saw Deputy Lance Cain walking towards him.

Cain stopped fifty yards out from Balum. They spoke no words to each other. The sun had drifted higher. The only thing between Balum and Cain was a thin film of dust hanging in the air, sparkling in the sun's rays.

Cain's hand dropped, and Balum's right hand palmed his revolver. As he drew, he rolled his left shoulder back, offering Cain a narrower target. The sounds of the two men's shots came so close together they sounded as one. Balum felt a tug on the back of his right shoulder. His gun bucked in his hand. He stepped forward. Cain had fallen, but from the ground he raised his gun. Balum shot again, and Cain's body lurched backward, the bullet slamming into his chest.

Balum holstered his Dragoon. The bystanders came pouring into the street to examine the fallen man. Balum's shots had both struck Cain in the chest, and the men took out silver dollars to see if they could cover the two holes with one coin.

Charlise was at Balum's side.

'You're bleeding.'

He looked at his shoulder. The bullet had laced the deltoid muscle along the backside. His shirt was ripped open and blood poured over the fabric.

'Come with me,' said Charlise. 'I need to look you over.'

Balum didn't argue. The adrenaline was wearing off. His head ached from dehydration and lack of sleep.

He followed Charlise back to the hotel where she led him through the door behind the reception desk. Cynthia was present, and when she saw Balum she jumped up to help. The two women fussed over him. They laid him face down on the mattress in Charlise's bedroom and took his shirt off and bathed and dressed his wound. He drank a glass of water, and before he could thank them, he was asleep.

He woke in the midafternoon. The belongings he had left behind were sitting by the bed, including his spare change of clothes, washed and folded. He put them on and slid on his boots and gun belt.

They had left a bowl of beef stew on the nightstand. It was not hot, but hungry as he was it didn't need to be. He washed it down with a pitcher of water. He belched and looked around. These women sure had taken a liking to him.

Cynthia was overseeing reception. She smiled at him when he came through the door.

'Are you feeling better?' she asked.

'I wouldn't say a hundred percent, but I do feel a might better. A bowl of beef stew will do that to a man.'

'Good,' she said, playing with her hair. 'My mom's out right now.'

'I'll have to thank her when I see her again.'

'You're leaving?' she asked, her face pouting.

'I'll be back to pick up my kit. Right now I have some affairs that need tending to.'

Cynthia crossed her arms across her cleavage and watched him go.

The townsfolk were riled up. It didn't take long for them to surround Balum on Main Street. Doug Bennett was one of the first miners to stake a claim in Bette's Creek and he had made friends. The news of his murder had them all tied up in knots. They looked to Balum for answers.

Balum hushed them. When they had quieted down he projected his voice over the crowd. He asked a few basic questions and got some answers in return.

Had the sheriff returned yet? No.

Did anyone know when he might? No.

Was Deborah around? Yes.

Where? In her house.

Balum squinted at them under the glare of the afternoon sun. 'The person who murdered your friend is relaxing in her home? And no one is doing a thing about it?'

'Ain't none of us lawmen,' spoke up a shopkeeper. 'We ain't sure how to go about it.'

'Same way as you would any other murderer.'

'Yes, but...her being a lady and all...'

'There's no cause to mistreat her,' said Balum. 'But you do want justice served, don't you? I'll go to her house myself. I just ask for a few volunteers to accompany me, make sure everybody knows this is on the up and up.'

'What will we do with her once we have her?'

'Put her in jail.'

'Then what?'

Balum glanced at the newly constructed gallows at the far end of the street. 'She'll get what comes to any thieving murderer. You folks have been itching for a hanging. You'll get one. Two for that matter. Soon as that would-be sheriff gets back we'll hang the both of them together.'

19

It didn't take any haranguing to rustle up volunteers. Balum chose the first three who raised their hands and they set foot to the DeLace's home.

He hesitated before rapping his knuckles on the door. He remembered all too well the look of that Colt Walker revolver and its nine inch barrel. He'd been shot once today, and that was already more lead than he fancied absorbing.

He knocked and quickly sidestepped. The men behind him did the same, suddenly realizing what they had signed up for. Women were treated with respect in the West. They could get away with most things. This was different though. She had stolen from a respected man, and killed him.

Balum knocked again but received no answer. Impatient, he tried the doorknob. It was locked. He took a step back, lifted a foot, and smashed his boot into the door alongside the knob. It flew open and he darted inside.

She was seated at the kitchen table. A cup of tea on

a saucer steamed in front of her. She looked up at Balum, her face shocked and blank.

'Hello Deborah. Seems you weren't expecting company.'

She stared at him and the three men in tow.

'Go ahead, finish your tea. I wouldn't begrudge you that much.'

The men led her from her house, through the streets, up to the jail. In the few minutes since Balum had addressed the crowd, it seemed the news had spread throughout the entire town. Not only would they be getting their hanging, but a double hanging, and a woman at that!

Pedestrians halted in their tracks. Folks came out from the stores and saloons and eating halls to have a look at her procession toward the town jail. They were silent. Somber.

The men took the keys from the wall and opened the very cell where Balum had been jailed. The cell bars closed behind her. They hung the keys back on the wall and filed out the door. Balum was the last to leave. Just as he was about to step through the door he heard that nasally whine that he had come to relish.

'Balum!'

He turned around. Her hands gripped the bars. Her beautiful face rested between them. She stared at him with frightened eyes.

Their gazes locked onto one another's briefly, and Balum tipped his hat and left.

Two men stayed behind as sentries. The DeLaces

had not made many friends in town, but there was no need to be careless.

The sun had set. Balum felt the heaviness in his eyes. A few hours' sleep in the afternoon and some food and water and helped a lot, but he was still a night's sleep away from where he wished to be.

He made his way back to Charlise's. He needed to pick up his belongings once and for all. He didn't relish sleeping under the stars tonight. Maybe old Chester would allow him to spread out on the hay bales in the stable.

She smiled at him when he came through the doors. She looked fresh, her face healthy in color and her silky hair falling over her shoulders onto her gigantic tits.

'Hello, Balum. I hear you've got her locked away.'

'Yes, ma'am.'

'People haven't seen this much excitement in years. No one has left town; they're waiting to see how it plays out with the sheriff.'

'So am I, for that matter.'

She smiled at him. He felt his heart race. She was all woman, and she knew how to look at a man to make him lose his breath.

'I'll take my belongings with me. Too bad your rooms are booked up. They beat a hay bale in the livery any day of the week.'

'The livery?' she frowned. 'I think we can do better than that. Come with me.'

She took his hand in hers. It was soft. She led him

to her bedroom. It was dark, it being evening and with the shades drawn. She lit an oil lamp.

'You've been through too much to be sleeping in some dirty livery stable. Now make yourself comfortable. I'll close up reception.'

Balum stripped down and gave himself a rinse-off in the adjoining washroom. Back in the bedroom he crawled under the sheets and dozed slightly until he heard Charlise return.

She stepped into the washroom. Balum rolled onto his side and rested his head in his hand. He waited for her to come out.

When she did she was wearing a thin white negligee that ended just above her waist. Below it she wore matching white panties. She turned to close the washroom door, revealing her plump round ass to him. She crawled into bed then, her breasts jiggling, nearly falling out of the thin top. She laid on her side, facing him. Balum couldn't help but stare at her enormous juggs, stretching the negligee fabric to its limit.

'I never liked that rotten sheriff anyway,' she said. 'With all the commotion you've caused, the hotel has been booked solid. I don't think I'll need to send Cynthia to the Candelabra for quite a while.' She smiled and brought her face closer to his. 'I think I'm starting to like you.'

He leaned in and kissed her. She opened her mouth wide and received it, quickly letting her tongue slide into his mouth and over his tongue. He put a hand on one of her giant tits and massaged it through the fabric while he explored her mouth. She moaned faintly.

He slid his hand down along her stomach and into her panties. His fingers reached for her slit, and he caressed it until it became wet. Her moaning became slightly louder. He slid one finger into her vagina, then two. She bit his lip and he pulled away. He took his fingers out of her pussy and brought them to Charlise's mouth. She closed her eyes and sucked on them while she rubbed her breasts.

Balum slid onto his knees then and guided Charlise's head to his cock. He was only semi-hard, and she eagerly wrapped her mouth onto it and began to suck the length of it. He felt it harden in her mouth. She sucked more passionately, moaning and drooling. She put just the head of his cock into her mouth, and used her hand to stroke the rest of his shaft. Balum reached down and squeezed her hanging breasts while she sucked him.

With his cock rigid as iron she sat up and pushed Balum onto his back. 'I want your cock in me Balum,' she said. 'I want it deep inside me.'

She wriggled off her panties and threw one leg over his waist. With one hand she pointed his cock into the air and slowly slid down until it penetrated her soaking pussy. She let out a massive moan and gently began to rock back and forth.

Balum grabbed a handful of her ass in each hand and guided her along his shaft. She leaned over him, the nipples of her breasts grazing his chest. She bent forward and they kissed. Her eyes were closed and she moaned and cried as he began to pump her harder.

She placed her hands on the mattress on each side of his head and arched her back. Her breasts wiggled in his face.

'Suck on my titties Balum,' she purred.

He grabbed them and squeezed them, pinching the nipples in his fingers. He jiggled one in his hand and shoved it into his mouth. He licked her tits, tasting her sweet flesh on his tongue.

Her pussy was dripping wet. Her juices had soaked his crotch and thighs. He wrapped one arm around her back and with the forearm of his other arm, hooked the back of her knee. He drew the knee up, and having her locked securely in his arms, began to hammer his dick into her cunt.

She cried out, wailing, nearly crying. Balum felt her body tighten. She gasped and sunk her head into his neck. He felt her spasm as she orgasmed. She came all over his cock, her pussy lathering it with its juices.

'Oh my God,' she stammered. She opened her eyes and looked at Balum. He grinned back at her, still slowly pumping her cunt. 'Oh my God,' she said again. Her eyes widened suddenly. 'You can't cum inside me, Balum.'

'Where do you want me to cum?'

'Anywhere you want, just not in my pussy. Do you want to cum on my face? I know you liked that last time.'

'I'm going to cum all over those big tits of yours,' he said, sliding out of her and rolling her onto her back. 'Hold them up and push them together now. Yeah, just like that.'

She jiggled her breasts for him and he stroked his cock over her until his cum came gushing out, streaking across her tits.

'Oh!' she exclaimed. 'Oh my goodness.'

His jizz ran down the tops of her tits and pooled in her neck. She scooped it out with her fingers and raised it to her mouth, letting it ooze onto her lips. She licked it off and swallowed it.

'Now isn't this better than the livery stable?' she said.

Balum laughed. Charlise blew out the oil lamp and the two of them drifted to sleep in each other's arms.

20

The next morning found Balum walking down Main Street toward the jail. He carried a plate of eggs and beans, covered with a hand towel. It was the same fare he had eaten that morning with Charlise and Cynthia. They had insisted that Deborah be fed while in jail.

Balum didn't argue. He needed to have a word with Deborah. He also needed to get out of Charlise's kitchen before he felt any more uncomfortable than he already did. Charlise had made no effort to hide her affection for Balum, doting over him and giving him kisses at the breakfast table.

Cynthia sat with them, pouting all the while. She scowled at her mother every time she leaned in to kiss him. Finally she had enough, and voiced out loud how upset her father would be when he came home and found a strange man sharing his bed with his wife.

'He won't be back for another week. And you're going to keep your little mouth shut,' Charlise had said across the breakfast table. 'Aren't you?'

Balum knew better than to stick around. He had shoveled the rest of his food down his throat and excused himself from the table.

Outside of the jailhouse two men sat guard.

'We was wondering what to do about feeding this gal,' said one as Balum approached with the plate.

'Any news on the sheriff?' asked Balum.

'Posse come back not more'n an hour ago. Said they tracked you all over Hell Country, and the trail led 'em right back here.'

'What about DeLace?'

'Well Mister, word travels fast. He must have heard his neck is next in line for them gallows; he plum disappeared.'

'Thanks. Keep your ears peeled for any news,' said Balum, and stepped inside the jail.

Deborah was standing at the cell bars. She had heard the conversation through the door.

'You won't find him. He'll find you though, and he'll kill you. You'll die by his gun or you'll die by the rope, one way or the other.'

Balum walked across the jailhouse floor and up to the cell. He handed Deborah the plate of food. She stood with her arms at her sides, her face furious.

'Go on now, take it. No sense going hungry.'

She took the plate and set it on the cot.

Balum pulled out a plug of tobacco and watched her. She didn't look like she'd slept much. He nestled the tobacco into his cheek and tucked his thumbs into his gunbelt.

'You just might be right,' he said. 'I may die. Won't be by the rope though. That rope is for your pretty little neck. This town doesn't take to thieving murderers. Someone kills a man and jumps his claim, they'll hang 'em. Even if that means hanging a woman.'

'Damn you, Balum. Get me out of here! What do you want?'

'I want that gold.'

'That's my gold.'

'You stole it fair and square I guess, but that don't make it yours.'

'Fine. You want the gold? Let me out. I'll show you where it is.'

'Afraid I can't do that, Deborah.'

'I let *you* out!' she squealed.

'You did,' he replied.

'So what do you want? You want to fuck me again Balum? You want to fuck my ass again?'

The way her voice whined in that nasally way and the language she used, it nearly made Balum swallow his tobacco.

'I wouldn't mind giving you another ride.' he said, smiling.

'Come get it,' she said. She pressed her body against the bars. She pulled the top of her dress down and stuck out a breast. It protruded through the iron bars. 'Let me out and you can do anything you want with me.'

Balum took her pink nipple between his fingers

and pinched it lightly. She reached her hand through the bars and rubbed his cock through his trousers.

Balum felt his head getting light and took a step back.

'What I want is that gold. And you're not going to tell me where it is, are you?'

She stared at him silently.

He turned and walked to the door.

'You're horrible, Balum,' she whined through the cell bars.

Balum turned and tipped his hat to her, then stepped out and closed the door behind him.

The sun was on its way to midday when he stepped outside. He chatted briefly with the two guardsmen, but couldn't keep his mind too well on the conversation. He wanted that gold.

Deborah had said she could take him to it. That gave him the impression it was close. But where? Balum mulled it over. The most obvious place was in the DeLace's home.

As soon as the thought occurred to him his feet were already moving. He crossed the street and down the back alleys, up to the DeLace house. The door was still half ajar; it couldn't be closed after Balum had smashed through it.

He entered and looked around. Didn't seem to be anyone about. The kitchen was just as they had left it. Deborah's tea cup still sat at the table.

He decided to start right there in the kitchen. He opened the drawers and the cupboards, checked around the floorboards, in the pantry. Nothing there.

He moved through the small house and came up to Deborah's bedroom. He looked under the bed, in the nightstand, the closet. He checked the floorboards again. Nothing. An armoire with three drawers stood against one wall and he went to it and opened the top drawer. Inside were Deborah's undergarments, neatly folded. He saw a pair of panties that looked familiar and he picked them up. The same from the desert.

Holding them in his hand, some part of his subconscious told him to turn around. He did, and a solid fist smashed into his mouth.

Balum flew back against the armoire and Henry DeLace followed up with another blow to Balum's stomach. Balum keeled over and DeLace threw a downward punch that landed alongside Balum's jaw, sending him sprawling onto the floor.

DeLace took a step forward and with his other foot reached back. Balum saw it coming and rolled out of the way just as DeLace's kick came in.

He quickly got to his feet, but not before DeLace set himself and smashed him in the lips again. Balum went careening backward onto the bed. He rolled off the other side and put some distance between the two.

He drew his gun.

DeLace threw his arms up. 'I'm not carrying!' he shouted.

'That didn't stop you from beating the tar out of me the other day.'

Balum put a hand to his mouth. When he drew it

away it was soaked in blood. With his glance averted, DeLace took advantage to dart out the door.

Balum followed, running through the house and out the door. DeLace ran up the side alley. Balum followed. They reached a tee in the alleyway. DeLace should have turned away from the direction of Main Street, but a mule cart had just pulled up and blocked the passage. He turned the opposite direction and Balum followed close behind.

They came out onto Main Street, one right behind the other. Balum was gaining now. DeLace was a large man, solid as a bull, but that weight slowed him down.

When Balum got close enough, he dove into DeLace's back and they tumbled to the dust. Balum jumped to his feet and the sheriff turned over, his hands reaching upward as if to ward something off.

'I said I'm unarmed!' he shouted.

'I'm not drawing my gun,' said Balum. 'Now get up.'

21

The townspeople came rushing in. With so many out-of-towners gathered for the hanging, there was already quite a crowd of people assembled. They formed a circle around the two men, cheering and shouting encouragement to Balum.

Henry DeLace rose to his feet and the two men circled. They were both built tough, but DeLace stood an inch or so taller and outweighed Balum by at least twenty pounds.

DeLace was confident. He had already kicked Balum around in the street, and had just given him a walloping in his home. He came in boldly, swinging a right roundhouse to Balum's head.

But this time was different. Balum had not just fallen from a second story window, nor had he been sucker punched out of nowhere. This time he was set and ready.

He leaned back, letting DeLace's swing fly through the air, and sent a straight right into the big man's nose. It knocked his head back and Balum stepped in again, throwing another right to the head and following up with a left jab to DeLace's belly.

That jab stung him, and Balum came in with another. The second one knocked the wind from DeLace and sent him staggering backwards. Balum closed in tighter, pounding him in the head with his fists.

DeLace attempted to throw punches, but they had no force behind them. With a jarring right cross, Balum sent the sheriff to the dust.

The crowd was screaming. They had gathered for a hanging, and it was violence they wanted.

The sheriff lay in the street, blood dripping from his nose. Balum turned to the crowd. He urged them to quiet down so he could be heard.

'This man here,' he said, pointing to DeLace, 'promised you a hanging. Let's keep him true to his word. Tomorrow at noon we'll stretch his neck from the very gallows he personally asked to be built.'

'Hang him now!' shouted a spectator.

'No,' said Balum. 'We'll let him get acquainted with the inside of a cell first. And we'll give him a final supper. Tomorrow at noon.'

He didn't need to ask for help to jail the man. Several of the bystanders grabbed him up and led him down the street.

Balum's face was bloodied and his head had been rocked, but urgency dulled his pain. That gold was somewhere about. The longer it took to find it, the more opportunity it gave anyone else.

Walking down the street, he studied the situation. Deborah and Henry were in jail, set to be hanged tomorrow. The sheriff had been foolish enough to go back to his house, knowing the whole town wanted him dead.

Then it dawned on Balum. The sheriff wasn't a fool. He had gone back to the house for a reason.

Balum turned and made a bee-line for the DeLace house. The door hung open on its hinges. He had already checked the kitchen and Deborah's bedroom. Henry must have been present that whole time waiting for an opportunity to get the jump on Balum.

The house was small, and the only two rooms unchecked were the washroom and DeLace's bedroom.

Balum didn't waste time. He reached the door to the bedroom and opened it. On the bed was a saddlebag. By the looks of it, DeLace had hastily stuffed it with his most important possessions.

Balum opened it and went through the contents. It didn't take him long to pull out the bag of gold, still nearly two pounds present.

Balum nearly cried out loud. He'd been through hell to get his hands on this gold. He inhaled deeply and tried to push down his exuberance.

First thing to do was get the hell out of Bette's Creek. That was the right move. And there was no time better than now. Immediately.

Although all his better judgement told him it was

time to ride, he knew he wouldn't get into the saddle without seeing Deborah and her father hang till dead. He only had twenty-four hours to go. And of course, he couldn't discount one more night in Charlise's bed. It wasn't that often he got his hands on a woman of that caliber.

As his mind drifted to Charlise, it occurred to him it wouldn't be a bad idea to get back to the hotel. Stash his gold, pack his bags, maybe get fed and get his bloodied face patched up.

He took half the gold from the bag and put it in one pocket, and stuck the rest in the other. He looked down. If no one knew what they were looking for, it wasn't too obvious.

He made it to Charlise's hotel without incident. He walked quickly, took back streets, kept his head down. He was nervous the whole way. There were a lot of honorable men in Bette's Creek, and a lot of unsavory ones as well, and it didn't matter how upstanding you were when you got the smell of gold in your nose. People would do anything for gold. He wanted those nuggets stashed deep in his saddlebags and safe under Charlise's bed.

When he entered the door it was Cynthia overseeing the reception desk.

'Balum, how nice to see you,' she smiled. It disappeared quickly when she saw his face. 'Oh my goodness, your face!'

Balum nodded absentmindedly. For the first time in Cynthia's presence, his mind wasn't on the soft mounds spilling over her dress. He had to stash that gold.

He walked through the reception gate. As he brushed past Cynthia she reached her hands up to his face.

'You're all bruised up. Let me help you'

He grabbed her wrists and pulled her hands away from his face. 'Not now,' he said. He walked through the door leading to the women's living area, leaving her at the reception counter.

Straight to Charlise's bedroom he went. He closed the door behind him and grabbed his saddlebags from the floor. He took the loose nuggets from his pocket and poured them into the bag with the rest. He pocketed several as he did so; no reason not to diversify his risk.

He shoved the bag deep into his saddlebags then covered it with his spare set of clothes. Satisfied, he pushed his belongings under the bed and stood up.

For the first time in a while he felt relieved. The cuts and scrapes on his face didn't matter. With all that gold, nothing much mattered at all. Top it off with a belly full of food and he wouldn't have a complaint in the world.

He left Charlise's room and headed down the hall toward the kitchen. As he approached Cynthia's room he heard sniffling. The door was open and he slowed and peaked inside.

22

She was sitting on the edge of the bed, drying tears with a tissue. When he saw her he stopped in the doorway.

'What's wrong?' he asked.

'You,' she said, wiping her nose.

'Me?'

'Yeah.'

'How do you figure?'

'You don't pay any attention to me. I thought you liked me.'

'I do like you,' said Balum. He entered the room and sat next to her on the bed. 'I like you quite a lot.'

'The only one you care about is my mom. You're always with her.'

'She's taken good care of me.'

'I can take good care of you.'

'I bet you can,' he said, looking down at her. Her breasts rose up and down with her breath.

She followed Balum's eyes. 'I know you like looking at my boobies.' She brushed her hair aside and pushed her shoulders together. Her cleavage deepened, straining the seams of her dress.

'I do. I sure do,' said Balum.

'You can look at them,' she said.

Balum cupped a breast through the dress. He squeezed it and she bit her lip.

She reached her hand over to his crotch. 'I know you liked it when I sucked your penis the other night.'

'Damn right I did.'

'I liked it too. Who sucked it better, me or my Mom?'

'Well,' stuttered Balum. He wasn't sure what the right response was. He didn't even know what the actual answer would be. They had both been incredible.

'I bet my vagina is tighter than my Mommy's is.'

Balum couldn't wait any longer. 'Let's find out,' he said. He stood up and brought her to a standing position as well. He turned her around and untied the back of her dress and let it fall to the ground.

She had not been wearing a bra. Her massive breasts swayed in front of her. Balum knelt down and slid her panties off. He bent her over.

She stood with her legs straight and slightly apart, bent over at the waist. She supported her upper body with her hands on the bed. Balum, still on his knees, took her ass cheeks in his hands and spread them apart. He sunk his face into her pussy. He ran his tongue along the length of her slit, tasting her sweet juices.

She let out a gasp, and turned her head around to try to watch him. 'I told you you'd like it,' she said. 'Stick your penis in me, you'll like that too.'

Balum kicked off his boots and ripped off his shirt and pants.

'Turn around here,' he said.

She turned around and dropped to her knees. She put Balum's semi-hard shaft into her mouth and slurped on it. In no time it was rock hard.

'Get on the bed,' he told her. 'Get on all fours.'

She did as she was told, and Balum climbed on the bed behind her, facing the open door.

'Go ahead, Balum, stick it in me.'

Balum took his cock in one hand and rubbed the tip up and down Cynthia's pussy lips. He smeared her wetness across her inner thighs.

'Stick it in me Balum, do it,' she begged.

He guided it in then, first the head, then all the way down the length of his cock. She was right. Her pussy was tight like a vice.

'Ooooooh,' she moaned, and rocked back and forth on his cock.

Balum knelt behind her, not moving. He let the girl do the work. She bounced her ass back and forth, sliding her pussy over his cock. She moaned as she did so. Her tight ass cheeks bounced against his hips.

Balum felt his head getting light. He felt he was in a dream.

When Charlise appeared in the open doorway, he thought for a second it actually was a dream. But only for a second.

Cynthia and Balum saw her at the same time. Cynthia stopped her rocking instantly.

Just like deja vu, thought Balum.

Charlise stared at them. Balum's cock was balls deep in her daughter's pussy, and no good excuse was handy like last time.

'You better have a good reason for this,' Charlise said, scowling at Cynthia.

Cynthia started to tear up again. 'You've been keeping him all to yourself. I like him too, and now he barely even talks to me.'

'Well he's certainly paying attention to you now, isn't he?'

'Don't be mean,' sobbed Cynthia.

'I'm sorry, honey. I'm not being mean. I didn't know you had taken such a liking to Balum. I don't need to keep him all to myself if it means that much to you. We can share. Can't we, Balum?'

Balum nodded. He was at a loss for words. His dick was still hard inside Cynthia, and he gave her a pump. Cynthia grunted.

Charlise smiled. 'That's right. I think we've both taken a liking to Mr. Balum.' She walked around to the edge of the bed and leaned over. She took Balum's jaw in her hands and brought his face up to her mouth and kissed him. Balum's got even harder.

He began to slide in and out of Cynthia while he kissed her mother. Charlise disrobed then, and watched Balum fuck her daughter. She climbed up on the bed and kissed Balum. He fondled her tits and sucked her nipples.

'I want you to eat my pussy, Balum,' said Charlise.

Balum reclined to his back. Cynthia turned around and got on top of him and slid his cock back into her. Charlise moved to the head of the bed and sat on Balum's face.

Her pussy smothered him. He reached his hands up to her thighs and munched on her cunt. She soaked his mouth, his chin, his entire face with her pussy.

'Can I have some of that dick now?' she asked her daughter.

Cynthia dismounted and Charlise took her place on top of Balum. The feel of her pussy was slightly different, and just as rich.

Cynthia watched them. She had a frown on her face.

'Don't get jealous now, Cynthia,' said Balum.

'Do you like her better than me?' the girl asked.

'I like you both just the same,' he said. 'Here,' he took his cock and slid it out of Charlise. Then he got back on his knees. 'Taste how good it is.'

She took it into the back of her throat. Balum placed his hands on her head and shoved his cock deep into her mouth. She moaned and choked a little. He took it out, then grabbed the two women, putting them each on all fours next to each other.

He got behind them and fucked each one, alternating from one to the other. Just as he felt like he might cum, he would take it out and switch to the other one.

The room reeked of pussy. The scent intoxicated him. He leaned around as he fucked them, watching their massive udders hanging down, swinging between their arms.

Balum felt his balls tighten. 'Which of you wants to take this load?' he asked them.

'I want it,' moaned Cynthia while Balum pounded her snatch.

'You want Balum's load Cynthia? You can have it. See, I'm sharing.'

Balum pulled out of her and she turned around. He rammed his cock into her mouth and felt himself explode, shooting a giant load of cum down her throat. She took it, swallowing, never removing her lips from Balum's cock.

He took his dick out then and collapsed on the bed. Cynthia licked her lips.

Charlise leaned down and took Balum's still semi-rigid hog in her hand. She put her lips to the tip and squeezed the remaining cum from him. She licked it up and swallowed it. She looked over at her daughter, laying on her back with her tits jiggling on her chest. 'Are we friends again Cynthia?'

Cynthia laughed. 'Yeah, I guess so.'

Balum didn't hear. He was already asleep.

23

Another morning in Bette's Creek. Another day of the orange sun baking the red clay of the earth. Another day for the miners to toil their claims, their aspirations as high as the day they first arrived.

Balum stepped out into this day walking tall in his boots. The gallows built for him would be used to hang those who authorized its construction.

The town had awoken early. Today was hanging day. They had come in from far and wide and had overstayed their visit. They were itching to get their show, to scream and yell and recoil at the sight of death.

The wagons around the gallows had been moved in order to create a path through them. The hanging was scheduled for high noon. People had spread picnic blankets at the end of Main Street. They took the most coveted spots first.

The hour was approaching. The street filled quickly.

Balum walked through them, past the wagons and

up to the gallows. Doug Bennett had so many friends that it had been difficult to decide who would perform the hanging. The men had ended up drawing straws. One man would place the rope around the condemned's necks, another would read out loud their crimes committed, and a third would pull the pin that dropped the boards beneath their feet, letting them fall to their death.

The three men stood atop the gallows. Balum climbed the crude ladder and greeted them. They had strung the ropes and tied the nooses. Balum asked if they had checked the floorboard pin. They had.

The crowd assembled below could sense it was close. They began to cheer, and shout out demands. They wanted the parade of prisoners.

'Are you boys ready?' he asked the hangmen.

'We're ready.'

'I'll bring them out.'

Balum directed himself to the jail. With no sheriff in town any more, and Balum with the biggest ax to grind, the duties of leading out the prisoners had fallen to him.

The men sitting guard outside were somber. They rose when Balum approached and opened the door for him.

Deborah and Henry were seated in their cells. Balum took the keys from the wall.

'You're a son of a bitch, Balum,' said Henry. 'I shoulda done like Deborah said, and shot you dead.'

'Lot of things you shoulda done different DeLace.'

Deborah stood up. 'I wish I had killed you in the desert.'

Balum looked at her, then at her father. 'Same I told him goes for you,' he said, unlocking their cells. 'Get on now. There's a hanging to get to.'

He walked them out of the jail, their hands tied behind their backs, and paraded them up the street. Balum looked at the faces in the crowd. Chester was there. Elsworth the gold buyer. He recognized the waitress from the Independent, and some of the poker players from the Candelabra. Charlise and Cynthia, of course.

The crowd had made sure to equip themselves with tomatoes, heads of lettuce and the like. With unanticipated days having been added into their timeline, the produce was well into stages of decay.

They hurled the food at the prisoners. Men, women, the children as well. Deborah and Henry bowed their heads and hunched their shoulders, to no effect. They arrived at the foot of the gallows covered in juice and seeds and filth.

Up the ladder they went. They came out on top, standing with their eyes wide in their skulls. The hangman pulled the nooses tight around their necks.

The second hangman quieted the crowd. He looked down at the people and took his hat into his hands. It took him a minute to find his voice.

'We're here today to have justice served. These two, Henry DeLace...Deborah DeLace. They're killers. They're murderers and thieves. They killed Doug

Bennett and robbed him of his claim and his gold. Ain't no question. And so...they'll hang...they'll hang by the neck until dead,' he clenched the hat in his hands and turned briefly to look back at the two behind him. 'God have mercy.'

There was a moment after the statement where the wind stood still and the crowd silent. The hangman tasked to pull the floorpin hesitated, his responsibility heavy on his conscience.

Balum watched from the bottom of the gallows. Deborah and Henry had their eyes fixed on him. A mix of fear and hatred came from their eyes.

Balum rolled the tobacco in his jaw and spat.

The hangman pulled the floorpin.

They dropped and their necks snapped, and they were dead.

Balum turned and made his way through the crowd. That nugget he had given Chester for the care of his horse was about spent.

He'd told himself more than once it was time to get out of Bette's Creek. Well, he thought, spitting tobacco into the dust; time to saddle up the roan.

Made in United States
Troutdale, OR
08/23/2023

12329196R00084